GANGSTA'S PARADISE 2:

HOW DEEP IS YOUR LOVE

LATOYA NICOLE

Gangsta's Paradise 2: How Deep Is Your Love　　　**Latoya Nicole**

Gangsta's Paradise 2

Copyright © 2017 by LaToya Nicole

Published by Mz. Lady P Presents
All rights reserved
www.mzladypresents.com
This book is a work of fiction. Names, characters, places, and incidents either are the product of the author's imagination or are used fictitiously and are not to be construed as real. Any resemblance to actual persons, living or dead, business establishments, events, or locales or, is entirely coincidental.
No portion of this book may be used or reproduced in any manner whatsoever without writer permission except in the case of brief quotations embodied in critical articles and reviews.

DEDICATION

Gangsta's Paradise 2: How Deep Is Your Love   Latoya Nicole

"When I see your face, there's not a thing that I would change. Because you're amazing just the way you are. When you smile, the whole world stops and stare for a while. Because you're amazing, just the way you are." Bruno Mars

Miracle Monet Riley you are the epitome of pure awesomeness. Everything about you shows pure strength and perseverance. The struggles and wars you have had to fight hurts my heart terribly, but you tackle each obstacle with a breeze. The most beautiful thing about it all is, you don't even know you are fighting. Each day you wake up with pure joy and love in your heart. You stay smiling and laughing as if you don't have a care in the world. You have taught me so much and I am so grateful that God chose me to be your mom. Your smile brightens so many of my dark days. Your hugs get me through so many broken nights. Your kisses help me to keep pushing forward. You give me the will to do better. You make me better. You push me to be the best mother I can be, but most importantly, you make me a better person. I have more compassion and patience because of you. I have more sympathy because of you. I love more because of you. The world may not understand you, but don't you dare try to fit in. Ever. You were born to stand out. You are a piece to the puzzle and also the biggest piece to my heart. I love you so much and I will always strive to be better, for you. Love always your mommy.

ACKNOWLEDGEMENTS

Gangsta's Paradise 2: How Deep Is Your Love — Latoya Nicole

To my publisher and friend Patrice "Mz Lady P" thank you so much for believing in me. You push me when I think I can't go any further and you have helped me unlock talents I didn't know I had. I love you always.

Tanisha "Tay" Okechukwu my friend, my sister. We have been down like 4 flats since Westinghouse and nothing has changed. Since the day we met, you have never changed on me. You believed in me and accepted me for who I was. You never asked me to be anything else other than your friend and I will always love you for that. Stay beautiful, stay you, and stay awesome. I love you to pieces.

Joanna "Shorty Doo Wop" Wright we are all still missing you and still have hope and faith that you are found alive and well. Your family and friends love you and we need for you to come home. You have been gone long enough. I love you friend.

Zatasha "the book plug" Shiffer I love you babes. Thank you for taking a chance on me and being my new baby once you bring me back to life. Lol. Just want you to know I appreciate you and everything you do. You hold us authors down no questions asked.

TO MY READERS...

I just want you to know that I appreciate every single one of you. I wish I could call you all by name and give you a special shout out, but just know I love you all. Growing up I was always told, what comes from the heart reaches the heart. I hope that was the case with each of my books. I was a new author and all of you took a chance on me. I hope to never let you down and I pray that I have your continuous support.

PREVIOUSLY IN GANGSTA'S PARADISE

GANGSTA...

We finally made it back from Indiana and headed over to the trap to see if they had heard anything. We walked in the door and nobody was there. I needed to relax my brain so I could think, so I sat down and laid my head back against the couch.

"I hope this bathroom clean I gotta piss like a mother fucker." That's the side of Sin I didn't like, when he acted like a bitch.

"Nigga you need to be in there washing your dick off. You talking about the bathroom nasty and you walking around with shit balls on your meat."

"Shut the fuck up nigga." We laughed and I closed my eyes again. Seconds later, my damn phone rung. I see I wasn't gone be able to relax. I answered the phone and put it on speaker, that way I could talk and still lay back.

"G, where are you?" It was Smalls.

"I'm at the trap, why what's up?"

"Anybody there with you?"

"Why are you asking all these damn questions? Just come over here."

"I'm not there. I'm heading back from Woodstock." I sat up and opened my eyes. Nobody knew where me, Paradise, and Sin lived. Not even my brother.

"What you just say?"

"Look, your brother traced Paradise car and it was at some loft building in Woodstock. I didn't find Suave, but it's blood all over the place and the place belongs to Sin. I think Sin did something to your brother. Do you know where he is?"

"Yea that bitch ass nigga upstairs using the bathroom." I jumped up and ran up the stairs. The door was locked. BOOM. I kicked the mother fucker in.

SIN...

When I got done pissing I headed back downstairs to give G a bullshit excuse so I could get up out of there. I needed to get to my burner phone to send him a message about the ransom. When I got to the bottom of the stairs, I overheard Smalls telling him that they were leaving my place and I did something to Suave. I was pissed because I left my strap in G's car because I was only running in to piss. There was no way I could get pass G and make it to the whip. He would kill me where I stood. I ran back up the stairs and locked the bathroom door. I hurried up and climbed my ass out the window. There was no need to try and get my gun, I had to get the fuck out of dodge. G was highly trained, there was no way I would win against him in a gun fight. There would be another time and another place. I had an advantage over him. I had Paradise.

GANGSTA...

The bitch ass nigga had climbed out of the window. Suave was right all along. I should have known to trust what that nigga was saying. It was like he was a psychic or some shit. That nigga always been able to read people. If I had listened to him when he said Lil Frank was telling the truth, I could have put it together then that Sin was involved. Fuck. All this time, the nigga I thought of as my brother was the one crossing me. I had to find that nigga before he did something like kill Paradise out of fear. I also knew not to underestimate him, he was a killer like me. It was time to move different. I had to change everything up, because he knew how I moved. I had to get the fuck out of this trap house. I couldn't allow him to come back and catch me off guard. I drove off with murder on my mind. This nigga would experience a death like never before.

JOURNEY...

I was sitting at my desk trying to look up something on my father. I had never met him, until he showed up at my house. My mother showed me pictures, but at the time I didn't give two shits about his ass. He had left us. Even though my mom didn't struggle, I still hated him for leaving us. My mother worked hard and had plenty of money. I always got whatever I wanted and went to the best schools. Now retired, she had nice things, but I always wanted to give her better. That's why I was going to take my father up on his offer. A colleague of mine walked up on me and I hurried up and shut the computer down.

"Captain wants to see you in his office."

"Okay I'm on my way." Wondering what he wanted, I got up and went to his office.

"Hey captain. You wanted to see me?"

"How is the Jamison case coming along?"

"I'm trying to gain his trust. It won't be long though. As awful as his files says he is, Jamison is a softy for women. They are his weakness."

"I see. Just remember you are on a job and you are not dating him. Are we understood?" I caught the implication loud and clear. He was telling me not to fuck him.

"I understand captain. I'm meeting up with him later. I'm going to try and get him to open up."

"You're doing a great job, but if it gets to be too much, know that you can always pull out at any time. No one would blame you. They don't call him Lucifer for nothing." I nodded my head and got ready to walk out the door.

"Oh, and Detective Garzon, be careful."

SOMEWHERE IN INDIANA...

Looking over the body that laid before me, I thought to myself, somebody really wanted this young man dead. Bullet wounds to the head, neck, and chest. Dumped on the street and left there. I was off duty when I got the call. I had to come in because they needed the best. Taking one look and assessing the situation, I came to the conclusion that anybody could have come in, it didn't have to be me. It was open and shut. A lost cause. But after working on this case with this subject, I'm glad it was me. It bothered me that no one came forth and inquired about him. That led me to wonder what kind of life he lead and what kind of monster he was that nobody came forward looking for him. Looking at the close range of the shots and the locations, I knew it was personal. Whoever did this, knew him. It wasn't my job to know what he did for a living, but one could assume. I walked over to my colleague

"How are his vitals?"

"Right now, they are stable. There has been no brain activity or movements from him as of yet."

"Get him some more fluids going. I'll be back to run some more tests on him." I walked out of his hospital room. Mr. Jamison was very lucky he landed in my hospital. I was the best Trauma Surgeon in the Midwest. I didn't even think he would pull through. The gunshot wound to the head is what bothered me the most. It would take a while for him to recover, but he would pull through. I would need to run continuous tests on him checking for paralysis and brain damage. Both were very likely and a strong possibility. I would do everything I can, but as a doctor, I could only do so much. Wondering again if anybody would come looking for him I thought to myself it had to be somebody out there. He was holding on for someone or something. Nothing else made sense how he made it through this. In this profession, I have seen love work miracles. I was hoping this would be one of those times. My name carried weight. I didn't like to lose patients and I was going to try my best to keep it that way.

1- PRAYERS

"I fear that what I'm saying won't be heard until I'm gone, but it's all good cause I really didn't expect to live long. So, if it takes for me to suffer, for my brother to see the light, give me pain until I die, but please Lord treat him right." DMX

GANGSTA

Mother fuckers got me fucked up if they think I'm going out like Willie lump lump. I have been out here nonstop, beating these streets trying to find Paradise and my big brother Suave. I could feel myself losing it and the only person that has been able to keep me sane is Journey. It's been 3 months since my brother disappeared and 4 since Sin bitch ass took Paradise. There has been absolutely no sign of this nigga. I know that I'm not focused because my emotions are all over the place. 10 years of training to transform myself into the devil with no emotions, and now I can't control these bitches. The shit is starting to cloud my judgement right along with Journey, but I need her right now. For some reason when I am with her I feel close to

Gangsta's Paradise 2: How Deep Is Your Love   Latoya Nicole

Paradise. As I stood in our warehouse, I did something I never thought I would do. I prayed.

"I don't even know if prayers get answered from a nigga like me, hell, how do Lucifer seek help from God? I'm not about to pretend to be something I am not, we both know I ain't shit. I have done a lot of things in life and I don't regret it. All I am asking is don't allow my brother and my girl to pay for my sins. Bring them back and you can take me. I will say this though, I hope it doesn't take you long to make up your mind because while I wait I'm going to send you some company." I looked to the nigga that was standing in front me.

"I'm going to ask you one last time what is her address?" I went to Sin's mama house only to find out she had moved. Luckily for me I ran into her nephew. He didn't want to answer me so, I decided to help him decide on what was best for him at this moment. I grabbed my bucket of acid and started pouring it on one of his feet. The screams came immediately.

"You better tell me something. Right now you still have one good foot. You can hop to some pussy, but if I keep going you know how this ends. What is her address?"

"Ok I will tell you. Just let me go." I gave him the pen and paper and allowed him to write it down. Grabbing my phone I hit up one of the lil niggas.

"Go check out this address. I need to know if a lady name Ms. Franklin live there hit me back."

"Aight I'll check it out now." I looked over at him and he looked relieved. I knew then the address he gave me was legit.

"You look relieved. Why is that?"

"I gave you what you wanted and I have nothing to do with this. You said if I gave it to you that you would let me live."

"I am going to let you live. It just won't be here. Your ass going to live with the Lord." I picked up the acid and poured it over his head. I watched as the meat and skin from his face started to slide off. I was done playing games.

TANK

Everybody is acting as if I am crazy because I believe Suave is still alive. I can feel him. I don't know how to explain the shit, but I know he is still somewhere out there. I need to find him before it's too late. I hate Gangsta ass, but I know we are on the same agenda. He thinks his brother is alive as well. Maybe we are both in denial, but without a body I would never believe that my husband is gone. G better find Sin before I do, because there is nothing or no one that would be able to stop me from taking his bitch ass out. I can't believe Suave didn't tell me he was going there. We already talked about this and I knew that

Gangsta's Paradise 2: How Deep Is Your Love   Latoya Nicole

Sin had something to do with Paradise being missing, but these niggas keep telling us to stay in our place. I was right then and I know I am right now. I think it's time we get the crew back together. I know I am pregnant and I know Suave is going to kill me, but a savage is being reborn so that my family could live. I just pray I'm not too late. I looked over at the girls and they were all eyeing me like I was crazy. We were in mid-conversation when I zoned out.

"Tank, what the fuck are you thinking about? I wish Gerry ass could get me sprung like that. This bitch is gone." Shay attempted to make a joke, but I didn't find it funny.

"I'm trying to figure out why I wouldn't be fucked up. My husband has been missing for months and with the type of meat he has in his pants, fuck yeah I'm sprung."

"All we are trying to say is, maybe we need to stop assuming Suave is missing. It's been too long cousin." I guess Bay Bay thought the way she worded it would make me feel better.

"Maybe, you hoes should get the fuck out. I know this is not my shit, but the shit you bitches are talking, I ain't feeling." I stood up letting them know that I was done with the conversation.

"Bitch we done been put out of better places. You are being sensitive around this bitch and we being realistic. Call me when you need me. If you think he is still alive, then do something about it." Bay Bay was always talking slick. I didn't even bother seeing them out. The way I was feeling I would fuck around and slam the door on them bitches. They were right about one thing though, it was time to stop sitting around crying about the shit.

SMALLS

I see why my nigga got out the game, this shit will have your ass out here losing it. I been thinking about Suave and how he got up out this shit and came back to help his brother and got killed. I know I have to avenge him, but would it be at a price I'm not willing to pay? Will my family lose me behind somebody else shit? The domino effect. My girl Nik is damn near 8 months pregnant and I don't want her to lose me to these streets, but that's all a nigga like me knows. I'm trying to be the glue that holds everybody together when my ass just as fucked up. I lost too much, but I know one thing I won't lose anymore without taking some more mother fuckers with us. I just hope we all make it out this time. I know I couldn't wait for this shit to be over, I was tired of arguing with Nik about the shit.

"All I'm saying is, he has a brother and a wife. They can look for him. If they need you, they will call you." Now aggravated, it was time to end this conversation.

"When I met you, your ass was a rider. Where the fuck is that bitch at? I'm sick of this whining ass mother fucker who always want me in the house."

"I'm still here, but it's time to grow up."

"Bitch I am grown. I don't have time for this bullshit. Either get right or get left. That's my nigga and I'm riding. If you're against him, then you are against me. Think about that shit because I don't keep enemies close. I dead they ass. Now get the fuck up and go cook me something to eat. Matter fact, since you want to run your mouth so fucking much, come put it to use. Put this dick in your shit." I could tell she was pissed, but one thing about Nik, she never turned me down for sex. Walking over to me she got in position to take all of me in. To show her I was that nigga, I slapped her ass in the forehead with my dick. I was not about to play with her ass.

HARPER

"Excuse me Nurse Jenkins, have any family or friends come forward looking for my patient Kendyl Jamison?"

"Doctor Morgan, I am sorry. No one has come forward as of yet. Have there been any changes?"

"Yes, I am about to pronounce his time of death, but if no family comes forward I will have no choice, but to have his remains cremated. If it was my family, I would want to bury them properly."

"I would as well." I walked away from the front desk when the nurse called back out to me.

"Doctor Morgan, I'm sorry you lost your patient. I know how hard this must be on you."

"I'm fine. I just wish I could have done more." I walked back into the hospital room and looked at the body before me. Turning off the machines, I looked at my watch and pronounced him dead. I looked over to the RN that was in the room with me and called it.

"Kendyl Jamison, age 40 pronounced dead at 2:43 PM. If no one comes forward by tomorrow, order a cremation. I left out as the hospital priest prayed for his soul, while I silently prayed for mine.

JOURNEY...

I don't know whether I am coming or going lately. I had agreed to turn Gangsta over to my father, but my job was still down my ass. They wanted me to check in with results. Sitting here in my Captain's office, I have absolutely nothing to tell them. I know that I am going to lose my job, but I don't give a fuck. At the amount of money I am getting, I didn't need a job. Keeping up the charade in front of Gangsta was the hard part. I didn't even know what my father wanted with him. It didn't matter how I did it, either way I was crossing him. I just hoped Gangsta didn't find out before the time came. Looking at my boss, I started feeling sick. Excusing myself as quickly as I could without making a mess, I flew into the bathroom. Barely making it to the toilet, I threw up everywhere. Sitting here on the floor nauseous as hell, I prayed to the Gods above that I wasn't pregnant.

2- HURT

"Ain't a damn thang changed I still keep that thang right up under my shirt, better tell em I ain't playing because it's all fun and games until somebody get hurt. Boy you finna get hurt, murked, put him in the dirt, boy you better catch me first." TI

SIN...

I can't believe I let these mother fuckers get the advantage in the situation. I was supposed to be in control. I had Paradise. I had all the fucking leverage, but here I am hiding out like a scared ass bitch. I definitely won't be hiding for long. These niggas think I'm playing, but I'm about to start sending pieces of this bitch to them if they don't give me what I'm asking. I didn't want to kill her, but the plan had changed and I needed to survive. It was time to make some calls and set some plans into motion. One thing a nigga can't do is resist some pussy. I know how G operates and that is how I would get to him. I didn't want to involve my sister, but he always had a thing for her. It was the only way for me to get back in front of this thing. I grabbed my phone to call lil sis when Paradise started up.

"Sin can you please uncuff me for a minute. This shit is cutting my skin. I'm cramped up and would really like to stretch my legs. Please."

"Bitch you think I'm stupid? I don't have time for this shit Tic I need to think."

"Where the fuck am I going to go? You have the gun, please I just want to stretch my legs."

"I'll give your ass 5 minutes and then I'm locking your ass back down." I kept my gun pointed at her as she stretched her legs. Watching her walk around made my dick hard. I know I didn't need to be thinking about no pussy, but I been cooped up in this damn warehouse with Paradise ass and I needed to bust one.

"Come here." I said to her as I caressed my dick with my free hand. I could see the wheels turning in her head, but she didn't know if she tried to make one move I was going to blow her fucking head off. She walked over to me and I pushed her down to her knees. I grabbed a condom out of my pocket and slid it on. She deep throated me immediately. I placed my gun at the temple of her head just in case she tried anything. I was not about to play with this bitch today.

SMALLS

"I'm not understanding how I got a team full of niggas and nobody knows shit. All you thick neck ass niggas in here and nobody knows nothing." I said looking around the room as I addressed my crew.

"I want a location on this loose booty ass nigga and I'm not about to keep asking for it. You telling me I don't have one competent mother fucker on my squad?"

"Boss, we have combed these streets left and right that nigga somewhere with Osama Bin Laden chilling in a cave."

"If that nigga is in a cave then we are in the fucking caves. There should be nowhere his ass can hide that we can't reach. Get the fuck out of my face until you have something for me." I was starting to get frustrated and I needed this shit to be over. I know the nigga a fairy, but the bitch ain't flew the fuck away. He was somewhere and he was close. I know he is waiting and watching, but I was too. I would make him pay for what the fuck he did to my nigga Suave. I just needed it to happen soon before someone else got hurt.

TANK

I done called Suave phone so much the battery must have finally died. I cried as I kept dialing it back to back. I had no idea what Sin did to him, but I was convinced he wasn't dead. I needed to get off my ass and do something. I hit up the crew and told them we were headed to Indiana. I walked on the porch to clear my head as I waited for them to pull up. I have not spoken to Smalls or Gangsta. I told they ass don't say shit to me until they can tell me where the fuck my husband was. I needed answers and all this stress wasn't good on the baby. I needed to keep the baby healthy, this was all that I had of him until he returned.

"Hey, I can't go with you to Indiana. I'm too far along and Smalls would kill me, but here, you left your piece in there and I need you to be strapped." Nik interrupted my thoughts with tears in her eyes.

"You know I wasn't going anywhere without my shit, but thank you. I know Suave would be pissed, but I have to find out where he is. I just can't sit here and do nothing."

"I understand, just be careful." She went to walk back in the house and turned back to me.

"Tank, whatever you find out I need you to be okay with it. I can't lose you or have you falling apart. You have a baby to look after." I didn't even respond. Her comment kind of pissed me off. How do you expect me to be okay with any of this shit? If it was bad news for me, then it was flower bringing and slow singing for someone else. Bay Bay and Shay pulled up and I walked to the truck. Suave I'm coming baby, just hold on.

HARPER

Walking into my house, I made sure to put on all the alarms and I watched as the metal shields came down over the windows before I headed upstairs. Grabbing the Morphine bags out of my brief case I headed to my medical lab I had built on my premises years ago. I was 39 years old and one of the richest most successful doctors in the Midwest. I was one of the best trauma doctors in the world, but my personal life was nonexistent. I was married to my job and although I pretended to be okay on the surface, the stress of hitting 40 and being single weighed heavily on me. I was an average looking woman. Cute, but nothing about me stood out. Even my body was average, but I had a brilliant mind. Most men couldn't accept that. My Ex-husband was another doctor that was on the rise. Being with me made his career sky rocket. I loved him with my whole being. We were working on having a baby and I wanted to do a home birth. I didn't want the media getting wind of it and making my child's birth a gossip story. That was why I had the lab built in my house. I stood in the mirror reflecting on the day I came home to tell my husband I was pregnant.

I can't believe it has finally happened. I was going to be a mommy. All the way home I prayed it would be a girl. I knew Timothy would want a boy and name him junior, but I wanted a mini me. I ran up the stairs and approached his study. Ready to scream to him the good news, I burst through the doors only to find him fucking the woman I knew as his sister.

"what the fuck." He looked up in astonishment and tried to calm down the situation.

"Baby, it's okay. Miranda is not my blood sister. She was adopted." I stood there in shock because I assumed he would give me excuses and beg my forgiveness, but that never came. He just wanted me to know it was okay for him to fuck her because they weren't blood.

"Come here. No one will ever find out about this. You don't have to worry about your reputation. For once stop being Dr. Morgan and be my wife. Be someone that has fun and enjoy her life." He started kissing me and I have no idea why I let him. Maybe it was because I was being told by everyone I was too boring and I needed to loosen up before I lose my husband. I figured it had to be my fault. I was so into my job that I pushed him into the bed of his foster sister. I felt his hands caress my breasts as he kissed me. He walked me over to the bed and I kept my eyes closed. I was scared, but I was afraid of losing him more.

"Get on all fours and suck my dick baby." I did as I was told. I opened my mouth and his dick slid in. I had never performed oral sex on him until this day. I could taste her on him. I almost gagged at the thought, but I kept going for fear of him leaving. I didn't really know what I was doing so I allowed him to guide it in and out of my mouth.

"spit on it." I opened my mouth and brought up as much spit as I could and spit on his dick. When he put it back in, it glided with ease. It allowed me to enjoy it more. It didn't hurt anymore. He wasn't a big man, but my mouth

wasn't used to it. Right when I grabbed his meat to stroke it while I sucked, I felt her mouth go on me. I wanted to stop her, but it felt so good. It was actually better than Timothy's head. It was gentle yet precise. Rough, but soft at the same time. She concentrated on my clit while Tim was always licking everywhere, but there. I felt a moan escape out my mouth without my permission. Before I knew it, I was screaming and sucking at the same time. My husband was brick hard. I had never seen this side of him before. Miranda flipped me over and laid me on my back. As she went back to work on my clit, my husband slid his raw dick in her. I watched him fuck her like I had never seen before. There was no weak, dry, and quick pumps. He grabbed her ass and went as deep as he could in her. His strokes had her going crazy which made her eat me more aggressively. As if they both knew I was about to cum she got up and sat on my face and he slid his dick inside of me. First time in my life I wasn't worried about hygiene and fluid exchange.

"Open your mouth and stick out your tongue." Miranda instructed. Everything in me wanted to scream no, but I did as I was told and for the first time in my life, I performed oral sex on a woman. She rode my face like she was riding my husband's dick. We all came together. Seeing the look on my husband's face made me feel good that I had fully pleased him. I got up and went in the shower. After being in there about 5 minutes I went to go get my husband so that he could join me in the shower and I could tell him *the news about the baby. Him and Miranda were in the hallway talking.*

"Look, I told you to give me a little more time. You know I am only with her to make a name for myself. When I reach the status I want to be, I will leave her and it will just be me and you."

"Okay, I just hope it doesn't take long. I ain't trying to be eating powder eggs much longer. That bitch pussy was dry as hell. I don't know how the fuck you been fucking her this long."

"With a lot of KY Jelly and imagination. Her slow ass never even noticed I was using it on her." They both started laughing and I eased back to the shower. I just degraded myself to please my husband so he wouldn't leave and the asshole never wanted to be there to begin with. After I got out the shower, I waited until they both went to sleep and I went out to his car and cut the break lines and the gas lines on his car. They fucked with the wrong one on today.

I laughed at how good of an actress I was when the police came to tell me my husband and his sister was dead. They crashed on his way to take her home. The only thing I regret is the stress from the whole situation made me lose my baby. I vowed I would now be in control of my own destiny and fate. I walked in my medical lab and looked at the man before me. This man was the key to my happiness.

It was a fresh start. I would have my husband and I would get my baby. Kendyl Jamison was now mine and I would kill anybody that got in the way.

GANGSTA...

"This nigga think shit a game. I'm about to fuck his whole understanding up. He thinks he can move mother fuckers around and I won't find them, I am everywhere, it ain't a place in this world these motherfuckers can hide." I vented to Smalls as I drove to my destination.

"Nigga what you on? You can't be around here on no solo shit. That's what my nigga Suave did and look what happened. I'm not trying to be out here searching for your Prince looking ass. Nigga what the fuck made you wear all purple anyway? Fuck was you thinking?"

"Fuck you nigga. I'm fly as shit, but I'm straight. I promise you need to worry about the next mother fucker. Quick question though. Who plans the funeral when the whole family dead?"

"Nigga I don't know shit. Fuck them and a funeral. Suave never left a body for a mother fucker to bury." The nigga was right, I couldn't do shit but laugh. Thinking about him brought me back to my current mission. I normally didn't do innocent people, but it's going to be a family reunion up there at them pearly gates. I promised God some company and I always keep my word.

"Nigga I'm going to hit you up when I leave. I'm about to pull up now."

"Aight bet." I disconnected the call and walked up to the address I was given. I was happy the house was secluded and I didn't have to worry about neighbors. I knew she wasn't home because I was having her tailed. Grabbing my gas can out of my car I walked up to the door. It took me about 5 minutes to pick the lock. Walking in I poured gasoline over everything in that bitch. Coming back into the living room I looked at the pictures she had on the wall. I was staring at Sin's sister Sinay when my text alert went off.

Lil Keith: Pulling up.

Me: Aight bet.

I could have hid, but I wanted the bitch to see me. No games. I needed to send a message and I didn't have time to play hide the black nigga.

"Oh my God, Kenneth you scared me. What are you doing in here and what is that smell?" I walked up to her.

"Hey Ms. Franklin. I hate to tell you, but you are about to have a bad day." Before she could respond I hit her so hard her wig flew off. Dragging her to the chair, I tied her up. I left the wig on the floor because she didn't need it where she was going. Thinking I may have hit her too hard, I started shaking her to try and wake her. This old bitch was about to piss me off. I flicked her on her forehead and she finally start to come to.

"What is going on? Kenneth have you lost your damn mind? Your mother would be ashamed of you if she could see you now."

"Don't worry. You can tell her all about it, when I send you to the same place I sent that bitch. Trade stories of the day you met Lucifer. Now I only have one question and your answer determines whether or not you get out of this alive. Do you understand?"

"Yes, but why are you doing this."

"Fuck all that. Listen, your son took something from me and I want it back. I can't find him and I need for you to tell me where he is."

"I don't know. Oh my God. Please don't do this." I walked up to her and grabbed her cheeks with one hand and snatched her dentures out with the other hand.

"If you don't tell me I am going to take you apart piece by piece. You don't want that do you?"

""I promise I don't know where he is. Why are you doing this to me? I have always been like a mother to you. Whatever Sin is involved in, has nothing to do with me."

"See, that's where you are wrong. You raised his bitch ass, which means you failed as a parent. Your son crossed me, and I need to find him. The only way for you to live is to tell me where he is."

"I just told you, I don't know. I haven't talked to him."

"Well, I think it's time you said a prayer." Her eyes pleaded with me to let her go and I didn't give a fuck. Her son killed my brother and kidnapped my girl. Somebody had to pay. The only comfort I could give her was letting her know she would not be alone when she got there. I would go through his family one by one, until somebody told me where he was. Changing my mind on how I was going to take her out, I walked over and untied her.

"Mrs. Franklin, I bet it has been a long time since you got fucked haven't it? I think you should try and fuck your way out of this. If you can make me nut, I'll let you live." The bitch didn't even think twice. She stood up and pulled her clothes down.

"Turn around." She did as she was told. Bending her over I slammed my dick in her ass. She let out a gut wrenching scream.

"Shut the fuck up and take it." The screams stopped, but she whimpered with each stroke that I gave her. I tried to split her insides apart. I knew there was no way this old bitch could make me nut, but I wanted to punish her.

Pulling her hair like I was trying to detach her shit from her roots, I continued to assault her asshole. When the blood started pouring out, I decided that was enough of that.

"Turn around." When she faced me I pushed her head down on my dick and made her swallow it whole. As I slammed my dick in her mouth, I reached my hands up and dug my fingers in her eyeballs. She no longer muffled her screams. The louder she yelled the harder I dug. I didn't stop and until I felt them bust under my fingers. With my fingers embedded in her eyes I used them as leverage to pump in and out of her mouth. Now I could nut. As soon as I released, I dug my fingers out of her eyes and twisted her neck.

"Sorry ma, I lied." Getting up, I grabbed my lighter and threw it as I walked out the door. I stood there and watched the house go up in flames. I don't think Sin was ready for the kind of monster he unleashed.

"You wanted a war, you got one."

JOURNEY...

Sitting in the bathroom I couldn't do nothing, but cry looking at the pregnancy test that I held in my hand. I couldn't believe I allowed Gangsta to get me pregnant. I was smarter than this. I could go to jail if my job found out I was pregnant. I needed my father to move his plan along before I started to show. I had no idea what he wanted with him, but for 500k I really didn't give a fuck. I could raise this baby by myself once I got this money. I just hope this shit would be over soon. I couldn't allow myself to fall for Gangsta. He was a job and I needed to remember that and keep it in mind. I decided to call my mother because at this point she was the only person I could trust.

"Hey ma, can we talk for a minute?"

"What's on your mind baby girl?"

"My father came to see me." I didn't say anything else because I wanted to see how she felt about that.

"I know you are grown and you are going to do what you want, but you need to stay as far away from that man as you possibly could. Nothing about him is good. He is evil to his core and if he came to see you he is up to no good."

"Ma I know and I got this. I promise I will be careful. I just wanted you to know. I will be to see you soon. I promise it will all come together in the end."

"As long as you are interacting with your father, don't contact me. If you want to say fuck your life, so be it, but you will not say fuck mine. That man is no good and outside of you I hate the day I ever laid eyes on that man." Before I could say anything else she hung up on me. I cried because my mother was all that I had, but she will be okay once we get this money, we can move far away from here. I needed to stay focused on the task, so I picked up my phone and texted Gangsta.

TANK...

Me and my bitches drove to Indiana. I decided to check all of the police stations and hospitals surrounding the area where they found his car. I was getting pissed because we had no luck so far.

"I know that you don't want to accept it, but it may be time for us to grieve Suave. He hasn't surfaced in all this time." I looked at Bay Bay with fire in my eyes.

"I will not grieve somebody who is not dead." You can tell Shay wanted to stay out of it, but she spoke up anyway.

"Cousin this is not healthy. I know you love him and it hurts to let go, but it's time to start thinking without emotions."

"I will search this mother fucking city like a bitch looking for her nigga's password until I find him."

"This is the last hospital here. I hope you find what you are looking for. Come on." Bay Bay spoke with a softer tone and it calmed me some. I know they mean well, but I could not accept what they were saying. My soul told me he was still alive. Walking in the hospital I prayed for a miracle. Approaching the front desk, I took a deep breath before I asked the receptionist the same question I had asked a million times today.

"Excuse me I'm trying to find out if my husband is admitted here."

"What's his name?"

"Kendyl Jamison." It seems like it took her 3 hours to type in his name and respond to me.

"Yes, he is on the 6th floor in Intensive Care." I almost passed out because I thought I heard her wrong. She wrote out some passes and directed us to the elevators. My nerves was shot when the doors opened. It felt like the only sound in the whole place was my shoes hitting the floor. I walked up to the desk and no one was there. I looked at Shay and Bay Bay and they were smiling with tears in their eyes. A doctor was approaching the desk, so I decided to ask her.

"Excuse me ma'am, they told me that my husband was up here on this floor and I was wondering if you could tell me what room he was in?"

"What's his name?"

"Kendyl Jamison." A look crossed her face, but I couldn't tell what it was. If I was a betting woman I would have said it was fear, but I wasn't sure. I couldn't quite put my finger on it.

"I'm so sorry. I hate to be the bearer of bad news, but we cremated him this morning." I didn't hear anything after I'm so sorry. My heart broke into a million pieces.

"NOOOOOO. OH MY GOD NO. PLEASE NO, NO, NO, NO. HE IS NOT DEAD. HE CAN NOT BE DEAD. HE PROMISED TO NEVER LEAVE ME. GOD PLEASE NO." I could see Bay Bay and Shay crying and the Doctor was talking, but I didn't hear a word she said. The room started spinning out of control and then everything went black.

SIN...

I looked around cautiously before I get out my car and walk into my sister's house. I didn't tell anybody what was going on between me and Gangsta, I just bought them a new crib as a gift. I couldn't take anything to chance when it came to that nigga. Using my key, I walk in and my sister is sitting on the couch looking a hot ass mess. My sister was every nigga's dream in the hood growing up. She stood 5'5 with a petite frame, but she had curves. She had the grey eyes just like me and she always wore her hair in a mohawk. I don't know what it was about her that had all the niggas going crazy, but none of them wanted her more than G. She would not give that nigga the time of day because he was like my brother. She ended up fucking with some lame ass nigga from the East Side and got pregnant. Now that nigga is in jail and she is left to raise my 6 year old niece.

The crazy part is, she was actually holding this nigga down on a 10 year bid. I needed her to get herself together for my plan to work.

"What the fuck is wrong with you Sinay? Why your ass in here looking like Celie when Nettie came home?"

"I been calling your phone all day. Mama is dead Sin. Her house caught on fire and she was inside." It felt like my soul was snatched away from me. I know it wasn't random, Gangsta killed my mama. As the tears fell from my eyes I decided to tell my sister what I wanted her to know, but it would be my version.

"Sis, Gangsta killed mama."

"What the fuck. Nigga are you crazy? He would never hurt her."

"Yes he would. I didn't want you guys to worry, but me and him been into for the last 4 months. He crossed me with a hit and tried to get me taken out. He is still looking for me right now trying to kill me. I'm sure he killed mama because he wanted to know where I am. We have to stop him and I know how, but I need your help."

"You know I am not a killer. That nigga is the devil, he would take me out in a second."

"I don't want you to kill him. I want you to date him. You know that nigga always had a thing for you. All you have to do is accidentally bump into him and then hang out with him. Make him think he about to get some and I'll come in and deaden his ass before he could blink."

"I don't know Sin. Mama always told me don't allow the devil in your house. He only wants to kill, steal, and destroy."

"HE KILLED OUR MAMA. HE IS TRYING TO KILL ME. Are you okay with that? Hell you could be next after me, you know he doesn't leave loose ends." I could see her thinking it over and I knew I got her with the last part.

"Okay I'll do it. Just let me know where the nigga be." Trying to hide my smile, I hugged her and I left. I now have two allies helping me, there is no way I could lose this war.

SMALLS...

Tank have been ignoring the shit out of me in my own damn house. She act like a nigga ain't out here all day everyday looking for answers on Suave's whereabouts. I was pissed when Nik told me that her and the other girls went to Indiana on their own looking for him. We don't know them niggas over there. I know she thinks we aren't doing shit, but being stupid is not an option. I paced the floor when I heard her coming in the door. I opened my mouth ready to tear her a new asshole when I saw Bay Bay and Shay damn near carrying her in.

"What the fuck happened to her?" the girls looked at me with tears in their eyes, but nobody said anything.

"Tank, I know you went to Indiana and I need you to tell me what happened." Looking up at me I could tell it took everything in her to speak.

"I found Suave." What the fuck is she crying for then. Damn he must have been with a bitch.

"Where is he? Was that his blood we saw in Sin spot." She handed me a ceramic jar.

"He's in there." She got up and left without saying another word.

"Somebody tell me something. What the fuck she mean he is in here?"

"We went to all the hospitals and jails in Indiana and the last one they told us he was on the 6th floor. We got up there and the doctor said he had just passed, they cremated him this morning." Shay said now crying. I felt so much rage and hurt. I can't believe this bitch ass nigga killed my man. One thing was for certain, everything keep leading back to Indiana and that's where I would go to find out answers, but first I needed to tell Gangsta. This was a conversation I was not ready to have.

GANGSTA...

I was waiting on my people to give me the whereabouts of Sinay. I always had a thing for her, but I need answers. She was going to have to give me those answers. Time was running out and I was not about to lose Paradise. Of course, every time my baby weighed heavily on my mind I called Journey and asked her to spend time with me. She been kind of distant lately, but I needed her right now. Sitting outside her house waiting on her to come out, Smalls hit my phone.

"Hey I need for you to meet me at my crib right now, I'll be outside."

"What's up nigga? What's going on?"

"G, just get here right now." And he hung up. That ain't like that nigga, he usually cracks a joke or something. I didn't want Journey to change her mind about kicking it tonight so I decided to take her with me. Once she got in the car I could tell she was in a shitty mood.

"Where are we going?"

"I have to go holla at my man real quick then we going back to the hotel. I just want to stay in tonight." She didn't respond and I really didn't give a fuck. I turned my radio up and drove to see what Smalls wanted.

Pulling up, I see he is already standing at the curb waiting on me. The nigga didn't even allow me to get out the car before he started talking. Now I know something is wrong because he knows we don't do this shit. He looked dead at Journey and didn't even address her ass.

"Hey nigga it's all bad. Nigga it's fucked up. Tank and her crew went to Indiana looking for Suave." I cut him off because I felt my anger rising. I was getting tired of Gladys Knight and her Pips. These bitches was always doing some shit they didn't have no business doing.

"Tank is not going to be happy until I really fuck her ass up."

"Listen nigga. They found Suave." I had the dumbest look on my face. You could have bought me for a fucking penny. These bitches did something a whole crew hadn't done.

"Where is he."

"He in the house." I opened the door to jump out to go see where the fuck he been, but Smalls slammed my door shut.

"What the fuck you doing nigga. Move the fuck out the way."

"G, listen man. I just need you to listen." I could now see the tears in his eyes.

"I'm listening nigga, but you ain't saying shit."

"When they got there he was already gone. He died yesterday and they cremated him this morning. I'm sorry G, but our nigga is gone." I waited on this nigga to start laughing telling me this was a sick joke, but it never came. All the fuck I saw was tears.

"Nigga what. WHAT? AIN'T NO FUCKING WAY MAN. AINT NO WAY." I no longer had anybody. Everybody I had was gone. They say real niggas don't cry, but I couldn't stop the mother fuckers from falling. We all assumed he was dead, but there was that hope that he was still alive. Now it was official. My big brother was dead.

"G, go in the house. I will drive her home and you can go meet up with her later. We all need to be together right now." Usually I would have some slick shit to say, but I just got out of the car and went in his house. I don't even know how I got in there. It felt like my legs weren't even moving. Tank and her crew were sitting in the front room. The minute she saw me she started crying harder.

"Tank, I'm sorry sis. I swear I am so sorry. I didn't mean for any of this to happen. He was all I had left. Now I have nothing." I grabbed the urn and sat on the floor holding it as I cried. Shockingly, Tank walked over and sat next to me. Putting her arms around me she broke down my walls I had up against her.

"You have me and the baby. A piece of your brother is still here. He will live on." I hugged her back and we sat there and cried together. We sat there hugged up until we heard Smalls crack a small joke.

"Yall niggas ugly as shit right now. Naw, but I am glad you all finally connected. We need to come together right now." Tank stood up and addressed the room.

"I know that we all have had our differences and the men wanted us nowhere near this situation, but as you can see we have been getting results. From this day forward, we all will work together as a team. Before Suave…" She got choked up and had to gather herself to finish talking. "Before Suave left us, I told him that Sin was involved and I was right. I tracked the car to Sin's loft. Me and my crew just found Suave. We took out a group of niggas that held you hostage, and we robbed a king pin by ourselves and walked away with millions. We are not bitches that are out of line and don't know what they are doing. We will find Paradise and we are going to bring her back. We will also find Sin and he will experience a death like he has never seen before. We have to work together because I refuse to bury or lose anyone else. Are we all clear?" I knew she was speaking to me. I was the only one who didn't want their help, but she was right. It was time for me to put my ego to the side. It was time to go to war.

JOURNEY…

I didn't know what to say or do when Gangsta's friend told him his brother was dead. I felt out of place and I just sat there looking in horror. I was happy at first when his friend offered to take me home, because I didn't have the slightest idea on what to say to G. Once we got in the car, the ride was awkward as hell. His rude ass didn't say one word to me accept what's my address. He got on the phone informing someone else on what happened. When he pulled up, the mother fucker didn't even look at me. As soon as I got out he drove off. That was fine with me though because I'm not trying to be a part of their circle. I had no intentions on seeing him ever again or G for much longer. I didn't expect to him to come over tonight after the news he just received, so I jumped in the shower and prepared to read a new book *by J'Diorr called Can't compete where you don't compare.* As soon as I laid down and grabbed my kindle, my door bell rung. I got up and opened the door. There he stood looking broken and depressed. He grabbed me and lifted me around his waist. Once he slid his tongue in my mouth, I instantly got wet. Leaning me against the wall he pulled my gown over my head. While sucking my breasts, he slid his finger into my wet spot. When he started playing with my clit I almost came right then. Lifting me up to his shoulders he slid his tongue up and down my slit. He was eating me so passionately as if he was in love, but when I looked down at him, he was crying. I didn't know how to respond or what to do, so I allowed him to do his thing. Carrying me to the bed he laid me down. Kissing me with more force this time, his tears dripped down to my face. He finally sat up and got ready to penetrate me. Grabbing me by my ankles, he pushed my legs all the way back until my toes were touching the mattress. Finally, he slid it inside of me. There was no love making, but it wasn't rough either. I couldn't explain it, but it was as if our souls connected in that moment. With each stroke I felt all of his pain, but I felt the pleasure he was giving me. Every time he pulled back he would allow his dick to slide out and rub it against my clit, and then slide it right back in. It seemed like with each stroke a tear drop fell from him onto me. I never had a man cry while having sex with me and it turned me on so much that I ended up squirting. This was the first time I ever did that without it being extremely rough. The wetter it got, the faster his pace got. Lifting my ass in the air he went balls deep inside my pussy. Using my breasts as leverage his strokes got faster and harder. I knew he was about to cum because his body started jerking. He didn't moan and grunt like he usually does. He released his nut in me and rolled over. Laying on his back, I watched him silently cry himself to sleep. Knowing that I was about to cause him more pain in his life, I fell asleep feeling like shit.

3- MY LIFE

"And I'm grinding til I'm tired, cause they said you aint grinding til you tired. So I'm grinding with my eyes wide, hoping to find a way through the day, a light for the night. Dear Lord you have took so many of my people I'm just wondering why you haven't taken my life? What the hell am I doing right?" The Game

HARPER...

I was reading a book to Kendyl when I saw him stirring. I got up and checked his vitals, when his eyes opened. It felt so good to know that I was able to love him back to life when no one else would. I couldn't believe that bitch of his thought she was going to walk in there and claim him now after all this time. Where the fuck was she when he kept coding. Where the fuck was she when he needed to be willed back. She was nowhere to be found and I wasn't going to allow her to come in now and take what I worked so hard to get. I went in on the overnight shift and I switched bodies. I paid a guy in the morgue to help me. We used a guy that had just passed and switched him with Kendyl. I inserted some meds in him to make him stay in a comatose state and hooked him up to the life support machines to keep him alive long enough for me to pronounce him. We then brought Kendyl back to my place and he has been here ever since. This stunt I pulled cost me 100k and I be damned if I let some hood rat ruin it. Now it was time to put my doctor hat down and put on my actress hat. I needed him to believe everything I was about to tell him.

"Oh my God Kendyl, I can't believe you are finally woke. God has really answered my prayers. I have missed you so much."

"Who the fuck are you and where am I?"

"Honey, don't use that kind of language. It's supposed to be a happy reunion. I have been by your side praying for you and loving on you and this is how you talk to me."

"Lady I have no idea who you are. Where is my wife? I need to get the fuck out of here."

"What are you talking about? I am your wife."

"What? Lady I think I would know who my wife is. Where is Tank?"

"I have no idea who Tank is. I am your wife and it hurts to know that the entire time I have been here willing you back to life, you were dreaming about some bitch. I am Harper. We have been married for 3 years now. Our house was robbed and you were shot and left for dead. They set it on fire with you in it. I came home in enough time to save you. Thank God you are married to the best damn doctor in the States. Now I know it's common for coma patients to dream the entire time they are out and that's the only reason I am going to let you off the hook. Whatever you were thinking, it was all a comatose dream. You have been out for 5 months." I could tell he was confused and had no idea of what I was saying.

"I have a brother. Kenneth. We were looking for his girl Paradise. I found her and his best friend shot and tried to kill me. I live in Hawaii with my wife Tank. She is pregnant." I started fake crying on the nigga.

"Baby listen to yourself. Do you see how farfetched that sounds? It was all a part of your coma. You dreamed all of that. You don't have a brother. You were an only child. Your mother and father died in a car crash 2 years ago. You are in real estate and have been for years now. You own property and you sell property. I can't believe my own husband don't remember me after everything I have been through." I started crying harder and I could see he began to soften up.

"I'm sorry I don't remember. All I remember is that. I guess it's because I have been dreaming it for 5 months straight. I'm not trying to hurt you I am trying to remember."

"I can help you if you like. I know every detail of your life. When you start to feel better, I will take you to see a psychiatrist. They can help trigger memories. Don't worry, for now just rest. I thought I lost you, I'm just glad to have you back." I walked over and hugged him and kissed him on the lips. He hesitated at first, but he loosened up and allowed me to. I walked out of the room feeling hopeful, but for now I would still lock the door just in case he tried something.

SUAVE...

What in the entire fuck is going on? Everything I know as my life is a dream? This shit doesn't make any sense. It all seemed so real. I still smell Tank? I know her scent, her touch, and I could feel her. How could I not know my own damn wife, but have created a whole wife in my head? I pretended to be sleep because I needed to process this shit and I didn't want to keep hearing her voice. Her shit annoying as fuck. Like one of them mother fuckers that always sound condescending. How the hell could I marry someone like that. She's not even all that attractive. She looks like life hasn't been all that good to her, but if her husband almost died I can see why. I opened my eyes to look around the room again and I notice it looks like a hospital, but I can tell that it is not. I have so many questions, but looking at her kind of creeps me the fuck out. I had to have a phone, when she comes back in I will ask her for it. My contacts would tell me what I need to know. I don't think she would make all of this up, but this shit was fucking crazy. I'm a boring ass real estate agent and my ass sitting here thinking I'm a king pin. I couldn't do shit but laugh at that. At least I dream big. I wonder what made me fall for her though. I don't know my type, but she definitely doesn't seem to be it. I am not attracted to her at all. Nothing about her turns me on. The bitch looks stiff as a nigga jeans used to be after using stay flo. One thing I do know is I didn't want to hurt her. I guess I had to try to figure out how to love her again. If I did it once, I could do it again. The shit was going to be hard as fuck though. How my bitch gone be walking around in some easy spirits gym shoes. Some shit was gone have to change.

TANK...

"Can I tell you guys something without you thinking I'm crazy?" Everyone was over Small's and Nik's crib. We were trying to figure out our next move.

"Don't try to come up with some rah rah ass plan sis. You and the Supremes get shit done, but yall be doing some reckless ass shit." Of course Gangsta spoke up. I know it's killing him to let us in on the shit.

"That is not what I was about to say. I know it seem crazy, but I don't think Suave is dead." The looks on their faces told me exactly what they were thinking.

"Sis, your ass is bat shit crazy. You been out there smoking with my baby mama? You know I ain't shit. If you are I will serve your ass, so get all your work from me okay?" Smalls said it like he was joking, but I know he was dead ass. He still serves his baby mama still to this day and won't accept any shorts.

"I know you guys won't understand, but me and Suave souls met the first time we laid eyes on each other. The day he went to see Sin, I knew something was wrong. I couldn't sleep it ate at me all night. Same thing happened to me yesterday. Out of nowhere I could feel him. I could feel his presence."

"Hey Suave, you my nigga and I miss you, but I don't do ghosts and shit. I will light your ass up in this mother fucker. Better take that shit back to Hawaii. Matter fact sit the urn on the back porch. Yall got me fucked up. Nigga not even welcome here no more. You telling me I'm walking around with my dick swinging and this nigga around here just looking. Fuck that." The nigga actually looked around like he was going to be able to see him.

"Not like that fool. It was like our souls reconnected. I could just feel him. I don't know how to explain it, but he is not dead." Gangsta looked at me with tears in his eyes.

"Sis, nobody wants to believe you more than me, but he is gone and that's on me. I have to live with that guilt for the rest of my life. All I can do now is avenge him. The person responsible will pay. I promise." He walked over and hugged me. Seems like that's all me and him do now.

"Gangsta you think Suave ghost gone fuck you up for hitting Tank in her mouth that day?" We all laughed because this nigga was stuck on this ghost shit.

"Smalls when are you going to Indiana and who are you taking with you?"

"I'm going as soon as I get this mother fucking urn out my house. A few niggas from the crew gone head out with me. G is going to Woodstock to see if the dumb ass nigga went back there. We will hit yall up as soon as we find out something."

"Okay, everybody make sure you check back in 3 hours. If I don't hear from yall in that time me and my crew coming and yall know how we coming."

"Okay Cleo, don't come set it off. Yall know Nik is TT her scary ass aint gone do shit." We laughed and they headed out. I went to my room and closed the door. Pulling out my phone I called Suave. Straight to voicemail again. Come on baby where are you. They think I am crazy, but I can feel you. Come home.

GANGSTA...

Leaving out I decided to drive through the hood just to see who was out on the block. I hadn't been through there in a while because I didn't want to give Sin's ass an advantage. When I got to the block I saw something that peaked my interest. What the fuck was she doing over here? I pulled up and let down my window.

"What brings Ms. Sinay to the ghetto?"

"Shut up fool. Have you seen my brother? I have something important to tell him and I haven't seen or heard from him in months."

"I haven't. I been looking for him myself. What's wrong?"

"I don't really want to talk about it." She dropped her head and wiped her eyes. It was in that moment that I realized I still had a thing for her. I just wanted to hug her and make her better.

"Get in the car. I was on my way to our old town to look for him. You can ride with me." I could see her hesitate, but she walked to my car and got in. Once I started driving I looked over to her and my heart melted.

"Now are you going to tell me what's wrong with you?"

"My mama is dead and Sin doesn't know yet. She died in a house fire." When the tears started pouring down her eyes I felt like shit. Not because I killed their mama, but because I was sitting here comforting her knowing I was the one that did it.

"I'm sorry to hear that baby. If you need anything I got you. All you have to do is ask."

"Thank you. That means a lot to me. You were always like family."

"You know I wanted to be more than your family though. If you had given me a chance, all the shit I'm going through wouldn't be."

"If I had given you a chance, I wouldn't be going through the shit I'm going through either. I guess you live and you learn. Now it's too late."

"Who said it's too late. I would drop anybody for you. You were the first girl to take my heart and you still have it. I love my bitch with everything in me, but I love you more." She leaned over and kissed me. My dick got brick hard. I wanted to fuck her right then and there, but I needed to get my shit together. We drove the rest of the way catching up on each other's life. I hadn't smiled like this in years. Too bad I was going to bring her more heartache. Her bitch ass brother had to go see Jesus and I was going to make sure he got there.

After we went to all the spots in Woodstock where the bitch ass nigga could be, we decided to head home. He wasn't as dumb as we thought he was. It didn't matter though because I didn't give a fuck if he was in Ray's boom boom room I was coming for his ass. When I pulled up to her crib I noticed it wasn't no rundown shit. It was a nice ass house. I looked it over and focused back on her.

"When will I see you again?" Can I take you on a date?"

"Yea we can, after all of the stuff with my mama's memorial service. We can't do a funeral because of the fire."

"Let me know the arrangements and I'll be there." I kissed her and got back in my whip. For the first time in a while, I was hopeful. I'm sure Sin ass wouldn't miss his mama home going. I didn't give a fuck what a mother fucker thought of me, if he walked in that door I was going to air that bitch out. Even though I was deep in my thoughts, I wasn't that far gone that I didn't notice this car following my ass. I pulled out my gun and waited until I approached a red light. Throwing the car in park I jumped out and didn't even wait to see what the fuck was going on. I started airing that bitch out. The driver was barely alive, but I only needed him long enough to answer my question.

"Who set you up to look into the eyes of the devil?"

"Nigga you have no idea. You think you are Lucifer, but you haven't begun to see Hell."

"Well, let me know how it is when you get there." I shot him point blank in the head. Jumping back in my whip, I got the fuck out of dodge. Did this nigga put a hit out on me? I couldn't wait until I got my hands on that dollar store sweet tart. He was really starting to piss me off. I almost forgot to check in with Tank ass, so I pulled out my phone and sent her a text. I didn't need her and her bitches coming through blazing.

Me: I'm good. Nothing there. Ran into some people on the way back. They singing in the heavenly choir now.

Tank: Glad you are okay. Let me know when you make it in.

Sorry sis, I wasn't heading in tonight. A nigga out here in these streets all night. When I pulled up, I got out and sat on the hood of my car. Something about the night air calmed me and I was able to think clearly. As I was sitting there thinking about everything that happened today, me running into Sinay and the niggas that was following me, I could feel my anger rise. This whole situation was starting to piss me off. Thinking of ways to calm down I looked up and I saw this bitch I used to fuck with back in the day coming out of the store.

"What up Tracy, come here let me holla at you."

"What's up G. How you been?"

"I'm good, but I would feel even better if you gave me some top."

"You miss me huh. I don't know why you ever stopped fucking with me to begin with. Where are we going?"

"Nowhere." Right there sitting on the hood of my car, I pulled my dick out.

"Damn nigga you not gone even get in the car?"

"I need to think and I need to see clearly, plus bitch don't ask me no questions just come do it." She climbed on top of the car and spit on my dick and started licking up and down my shaft. 5 minutes later the bitch was still licking my shaft and jiggling my balls. Getting aggravated I grabbed her by her head and slammed it down on my dick. I kept pushing until I felt her tonsils.

"Bitch I said I wanted some head, not a damn tickle me elmo session." I let her head go and allowed her to do her thing. That was a big mistake. The bitch kept letting it out her mouth to look at it. I don't know if the bitch thought the shit was gone change colors or what, but she was getting on my nerves and I was starting to regret this. Grabbing her head again, I decided to get my own damn nut. I slammed her head up and down on my dick so hard I think my balls was starting to swell. I could tell the bitch was choking, but I didn't care. If she would have done it right I wouldn't have had to take over. She kept trying to pull away, so I stood up to have some leverage. Now I could get all 10 inches inside of her throat. I envisioned it was Sinay's pussy and I went to work on her mouth. I completely forgot she was even there. I could hear her trying to scream or talk I don't know what the bitch was doing, but I didn't care. The noises only turned me on more. I slammed harder and harder into her mouth. Next thing you know the bitch threw up on my dick. The shit shot everywhere, but I was about 20 seconds from cumming and I didn't give a fuck. Keeping up my pace, I slammed my dick in and out of her until I felt my dick swelling. I pulled out and nutted all over her face and in her hair. Using my dick to slap her on the mouth to get the rest of my nut out, I was satisfied and could now think with a clear head. I walked to the trunk of my car and pulled out some jogging pants. Using some baby wipes to clean myself off, I changed my shit right there. When I walked back to the front of my car the bitch was still sitting there with the throw up and nut on her face. She looked so fucking pitiful.

"Why the fuck are you still sitting here looking like chili and ranch dressing."

"I was waiting on you to bring me a towel."

"Bitch if you don't get the fuck off my car before you get some of that shit on my hood." She sat there looking at me in disbelief.

"Bitch move, before I drag your ass." It amazed me how hoes actually thought I would treat them like wifey. Looking at her with fire in my eyes, the bitch finally got the hint and got up. When she walked off it dawned on me that Smalls hadn't checked in yet.

SMALLS...

Once we got to Indiana, we rode around in the area the doctor told Tank they found Suave. It was the same spot we found his car. To me that means Sin knows somebody out here and he may be around this mother fucker. The only thing is, we don't know these niggas out here. I really didn't give a fuck how they were going to take it, but somebody was going to tell us something. I saw a group of niggas standing outside on the curb.

"Listen up lil niggas, we don't know these mother fuckers. If they blink wrong lay they asses out. We can't leave anything to chance. Are yall ready?"

"Fuck yea." Lil Goon stay ready. That's why I fucked with him. He was my little protégé. We got out and I approached the crowd.

"Hey, do yall know a nigga named Sin? If so, I got a grip for his whereabouts."

"Fuck is yall. Do we look like some snitches? Yall better keep it moving before I knock one of yall asses out." I guess this big ass Twinkie eating nigga was the leader. Nigga talking about fighting and all I wanted to do was give him my school lunch.

"Look, we ain't no cops and we ain't on no bullshit. I'm looking for my nigga. We don't know if he hiding or missing. Either you know him or you don't all the extra shit don't move me. Yall can make some bread, well you gone eat the bread, but nigga you get my drift." I could tell he was about to be on some tough shit so I prepared myself for it.

"Oh you a funny nigga. Let's see if your ass still laughing when I put you to sleep." He walked his big ass up ready to throw hands. I pulled my piece out and pointed it at him.

"Nigga I don't fight. Fuck you thought this was. I can see this is not going to be a friendly conversation. I don't talk well when niggas trying to make me they midnight snack. Gone and wobble your big ass over there before I make you shed a few pounds." I started walking off, but out the corner of my eye I saw his homie cock his gun back. I guess the big homie wasn't going to make it to dinner. I lit his ass up. Once I let it ride, all my niggas started letting it go. All the big nigga's people was firing too. We were in the middle of a shootout. I needed all my niggas to make it out alive. We headed for the car trying to find cover. Lil Goon was a hot head like me. This nigga stands up and started airing they ass out. I jumped up because I saw a nigga running out the house aiming his gun at Lil Goon.

"Nigga get down, but he couldn't hear me over the gun fire. As soon as I got to him to pull him down I was hit. The bullet ripped through my neck hot and fast. Then my chest. It felt like my whole body was on fire. I turned over and aimed at the nigga shooting and gave him a dome shot. Laying back down, all I could think was Nik was going to fuck me up. Everything was fading and I knew a nigga wasn't gone make it. My boys grabbed me and carried me to the car. I could feel myself on the way out.

"Call Tank." I managed to get out before I went to go meet my maker.

4- FAKE LOVE

"How you wanna clique up after your mistakes? Look you in the face and it's just not the same. I've been down so long it look like up to me, they look up to me. I got fake people showing fake love to me. Straight up to my face." Drake

PARADISE...

I been plotting for months on how to get away from this nigga. He worried about G, but if I ever get my hands on his ass, he is going to wish that G is the one that got him. I think everybody keep forgetting that I'm the one that taught my baby everything he knows. I keep asking him to uncuff me in hopes that he forgets to cuff me back. That's why I been obliging with everything his bitch ass says. I just need the right moment for him to fuck up. He been making calls all day. Usually after he is done trying to set up G, he be worked up and ready to fuck or want some head. But he usually keeps the gun pointed at my head so I can't take that chance. He is losing it and I know he will fuck up soon. I just have to stay focused and don't let this shit break me. He was walking back and forth pacing the floor while on his call. When he hung up he came over to me and I knew what was coming I was used to it now. This time I just wished he would put his gun down.

"You can't go and see him today. I'm not ready yet. Can't you stall for a couple of days." I could only hear his end of the call. I had no idea who he was talking to.

"Just give me a few days. I need to make sure my other people are ready. Tell him Friday. Aight." He hung up and began rubbing his temples. He uncuffed me.

"Stretch your legs and make sure you stretch them good because I need a good fuck. Not that dry stiff shit you been giving me lately."

"Okay. I been horny anyway. I will make sure it's good." I was trying to butter him up so that he could trust me. While I walked around I could see him rubbing his dick getting it ready. Every time he touched me I wanted to throw up, but this time I had to play the part. I had to get the fuck up out of here. I started this shit and it was time for me to put an end to it. I walked back over to him ready to put it on his ass. I needed for him to forget everything and everybody. I grabbed his dick and his phone rung. He walked away from me.

"What the fuck. I don't care what you think is best. I'm coming over. I'll be there in a minute." Damn. I guess I was going to have to wait until he got back. He put the cuffs back on me and walked out the warehouse. I looked down at my hands and I almost cried. He didn't slip up, the nigga fucked up. I had too much room in the cuffs. I could slide my hands out. I waited for about 10 minutes to make sure that he didn't come back in. I slid my hands out and I couldn't do shit, but cry. I couldn't even remember the last time I shed a tear, but a bitch did today. I got myself together and walked slowly towards the door. Peeking out I could tell he was gone. I took off running as fast as I could. After running about 15 minutes I could see I was approaching a gas station. A van drove right pass me, I couldn't even ask for help it rode pass so fast. Finally, I made it to the gas station and almost passed out I was so tired. I wanted to curse the damn people in the van out when I walked up and saw them sitting in the gas station laughing and chilling. Putting my pride to the side I decided to ask them for some assistance. I turned to say something when the passenger jumped out and put a bag over my head. I couldn't see anybody, but I could hear voices.

"Tie her up. The boss said to bring her to his house." Ain't this about a bitch. I finally escape after all these months only to get kidnapped again.

SUAVE...

Getting used to my real life was mad crazy. The only life that I knew was the one I made up and I didn't know how to deal with this shit. I asked her for my phone and she told me everything got burned in the fire. I have nothing that gives me a clue to who I am. She brought me all kinds of research on other people who went through the same shit as me, but it was pissing me off that every time I asked her a question or wanted her to clarify some shit the bitch got mad. How the fuck do you expect me to remember if you don't want to give me answers. That ain't what pissed me off the most though. She walked her ass in here trying to have sex and the bitch was wearing them damn Easy Spirits. Every time she would kiss me, my eyes would trail down to those shoes and I immediately became turned off. She had a physical therapist coming in working with me and the bitch was fine as hell. She fired her though when she came in and saw my dick was hard. Now I'm working with this nigga named Jose. She was happy because I was working with a man, but I was pissed because Jose was a damn fairy. I almost slapped his ass when he snapped his fingers at me and told me "You better get it together hunny. Your wife wants some of this meat and you have to be strong okay." I been working extra hard to get back right so he can go back where the fuck he came from. My attitude been real fucked up and I told myself I would do better and try to show my wife some affection. I didn't know the time would be now. She walked in the room in what I guess she thought was lingerie. Shit looked like a slip to me, but I could appreciate the effort. I was just glad she didn't have on them fat ass easy spirits. Walking over to me, she attempted to do a little dance and it took everything in me not to laugh. When she kissed me I allowed her to this time.

I even kissed her back. She was a bit aggressive, but I guided her and took control of the pace with my tongue and she caught on easy. After about 5 minutes she actually managed to get my dick hard. I grabbed her hand and placed it on my meat. She looked at me confused like she didn't know what I wanted her to do with it. Placing my hand on top of hers, I showed her how to caress my shit. When I pulled it out, I thought the bitch was gone pass out. She looked horrified at the size. Which was strange to me since we were married. Again, she looked lost. The shit was about to make my dick soft. She was too fucking old to not know what to do with a dick. Grabbing her by her head, I guided her down to where she came face to face with my meat. Of course, she didn't know what to do. She started placing dry ass kisses on the tip of it, while attempting to jag it off. Enough was enough.

"Open your mouth Harper." She tensed up, but she did as she was told. I slid her down slowly. Each time, I slid her down further than the last. I knew she was uncomfortable, but she would get used to it. Hell, she better get used to it if she wanted her husband to stay. When she least expected it, I pushed her all the way down making her take all of me in. I let her gag for about 10 seconds so that her mouth would be good and wet.

"Spit it out on my dick." Looking nervous, she spit all of her saliva on me and I slid her head back down. This made it easier for her. I let her head go and allowed her to do it on her own.

"Keep going and make sure to watch your teeth." It took me like 10 minutes to get into it, but she finally got it good enough to where it kept me hard and wanting more. Climbing on top of me, I held her up so that I could help her slide down on it. I could barely get the mother fucker in.

"Wait a minute, you gone scrape my shit up." Lifting her up to my face, dove in. I started slowly with her and licked gently up and down her clit. Her body shivered with each stroke. Wrapping my lips around her clit I sucked gently and she went crazy. Even though I was a beast at what I do, her pussy didn't feel like mine. I didn't know how to explain it, but I'm down here sucking for dear life and this bitch is still dry. Ain't no way my pussy would feel like some saltine crackers and my mouth is on it, but I said fuck it cus my dick is hard now and wasn't no turning back. Looking over at the medical table next to us, I slid my hand up there to grab some petroleum jelly. I squeezed some out to rub on my dick because there was no way I was going to allow her to scrape my shit. I slid her back down and this time I didn't care if it hurt or not. I pushed straight in and went to work. I didn't even give her time to adjust. I was over this shit and wanted to bust my nut. Grabbing her by her hips, I made sure she felt all of me in her stomach. Once I got my stroke going she started screaming for dear life. The shit was mad irritating, but I needed this nut. Pumping as hard as I could, I finally forced my nut to the top. Something in me told me not to nut in this bitch, but when I went to lift her up she locked her legs around me and started fucking me like I was the bitch. Where was all this movement when we were fucking. My dick had a mind of its own and before I knew it I had nutted. When I looked up the bitch actually looked satisfied. She climbed off me and attempted to leave, but this time I stopped her I needed answers.

"You say you are my wife right?"

"Of course, Kendyl. That question is starting to become redundant." She said with an attitude. I wanted to tell her no bitch your head is redundant, but I kept my cool.

"Then why aren't you used to my dick size? You didn't even know how to give head. You telling me we had sex for 3 years and you never learned?"

"This is the first time I ever performed oral sex on you and I'm not used to your size because I haven't had it in a while. You were in a coma, remember?" What the fuck. Ain't no way I was with a bitch and didn't get any head from her. This shit is starting to sound suspect. I decided to ask more questions. Red flags were everywhere now.

"Okay, you say that you keep me in here because you are scared that I will get shot up again, but you leave out every day. You aren't scared, but you think I am going to stay cooped up in this mother fucker?"

"Don't talk to me like that. If you want to go outside, we can go for dinner later. First, I am going to take you to see the psychiatrist. It's obvious you think I am lying and that shit hurts. I have been through enough waiting on you to come back to me and this is how you treat me. I will be back with you some clothes and shoes. We will leave then." Ignoring her temper, I continued.

"Get me a new phone as well. I'm sure they can restore my contacts. Them mother fuckers gotta be in the cloud." She walked out and slammed the door. I didn't give a fuck about her attitude. Shit needed to start adding up or she was going to have a problem.

HARPER...

Why the fuck couldn't he just accept the answers I gave him. We just had a beautiful moment and he had to fuck it up with all these questions. Hopefully, after he left my friend he would stop fighting this shit and just accept it. Praying that I got pregnant on the first try, I smiled at the moment we just shared. There is no way he would want to leave once he found out I was pregnant. I got in my car and drove to the mall to get him some clothes. He was going to have to look the part of a real estate agent and the husband of a doctor. Going in Ralph Lauren I grabbed him a button up, some khakis, and some boat shoes. Looking it over, I was pleased with the look. Then I went to Verizon and got him a phone under my line. Driving back to the house, I knew he wanted his phone to retrieve his contacts. I had a trick for him though. As soon as I got back I went into my study. Grabbing his phone out of my safe I turned it on. I was going to block all of the numbers he knows and add fake contacts and numbers into his phone. I would also call Verizon and have his phone restricted from dialing out to any number, but mine. As soon as I clicked on Tank's name, the phone rang.

TANK...

I couldn't help the way I felt. Everybody was walking around thinking I'm crazy and shit because I keep dialing Suave's phone. Something in my heart told me that my husband was alive and I didn't give a fuck who felt otherwise. Like I did any other day, I dialed his phone 10 times back to back hoping that it would ring. Just as I was about to give up, I decided to dial it one more time. I almost pissed on myself when it started ringing. The phone picked up.

"Hello. Hello. Hello. Is someone there. Can you please say something?" Then the phone hung up. I kept calling it back, but this time they kept sending me to voicemail. After about 10 minutes the phone started back going straight to voicemail. I jumped up and ran in the room with Nik.

"Hey bitch somebody just answered Suave's phone."

"Okay now I am starting to worry."

"Bitch I ain't that fucking crazy somebody answered his damn phone."

"What they say?" Her tone was starting to piss me off.

"Bitch they didn't say nothing they just held it and then hung up." I could tell she didn't believe me, so I pulled up my call log.

"Look at how many seconds I was on the call. Somebody answered. Then they kept sending me to voicemail. Now it's not ringing at all."

"Maybe somebody found it the night he got shot. Or maybe Sin has it." I never thought about that. I stood there in deep thought when my phone rung. Me and Nik looked at each other.

"Bitch it says the call is from Indiana."

"That's where you found Suave so answer it." I picked up cautiously. It was Lil Goon calling from the hospital telling me to get there right now. Smalls had been shot. I looked over to Nik and I didn't want to speak, but I knew I had to.

"We have to go to Indiana."

"Was it about Suave. What happened?"

"Smalls got shot. Get dressed." I walked off to go throw some clothes on and I called G and told him to meet us there. I really didn't want to go back to that hospital, but I knew Smalls needed us and Nik needed me more. Here we go again, I said to myself as I threw on some leggings and J's.

SUAVE...

I could have beat this bitch ass for the clothes she brought me back from the mall. I look like a damn teacher. Only thing missing was the Cardigan tied around my neck. Something is definitely off. There is no way I would wear some shit like this. I hope I wasn't this nigga. If I was, the shit was about to stop. She gave me a new phone, but for some reason it's not letting me dial out. I was going to have to wait until tomorrow to take it for them to fix this shit. The psychiatrist finally walked in and introduced herself to us. The entire time she was talking I was reading her and Harper's expressions. Everything she said to me was the exact same thing my wife had already told me.

"I get all that doc, but what I'm trying to figure out is when am I going to start remembering my old life. I feel like I'm trying to force myself to be something I'm not, but it's who I was. Shit feels weird as hell and she gets mad when I ask questions."

"Harper I know this is hard on you, but it's worse for him. Everything he thinks he knows about himself is a lie. You have to give him time to remember and be patient. You may hold a memory that could help him. Whenever he has questions, you need to answer them and give him space to accept them."

"I know that, but it just feels like he is calling me a liar when he doesn't remember." Harper had an attitude as usual.

"I will start therapy with him twice a week. We will do tests and activities to try and jog his memory. You both have to accept that his memory may never come back, but I will do what I can to help." I was not trying to hear that shit. I needed that shit to come back or I was going to leave her ass. Because the nigga I am today don't want her. We thanked the doctor and walked out. Waiting on the elevator, she seemed to be at peace. I was just as confused before I went in there. They keep telling me it's normal for comatose patients to go through this, but I didn't like this feeling. When we stepped on the elevator, Harper started pushing the button like crazy to get the doors to close.

"I'm looking for Matthew Davis room." I looked up because I knew that voice in my sleep. As the doors closed I saw her. I know I'm not crazy, but I saw Tank. If all this shit is a dream and none of it is my life, then who the fuck is Tank. Have I met her before? Is she somebody I fucked before in my past? Maybe I cheated on my wife with Tank. That is the most believable thing yet. I could tell Harper was watching me closely and I tried my best to play it off like I didn't see her. I don't know what the fuck was going on, but when they fixed my phone tomorrow I would call Tank's number and see who the fuck she is. I needed answers and it was clear Harper ass had no intentions on giving them to me.

The ride back to the house was quiet as hell, but I was done asking questions. I was going to figure this shit out on my own. Tank was somebody. Who she was, I don't know. My soul and my dreams tell me she was mine. Harper insists that she is. We got out the car and I couldn't wait to get the fuck out of these clothes.

"Baby can you come into the medical lab. I want to check your wounds and see how they are. We shouldn't have had sex on them that early and I want to make sure I didn't damage anything."

"Okay make this shit quick. I wanna get out of these clothes and take a shower." Getting up on the bed I laid back while she checked me. She raised my arms and then I heard the click. This bitch done handcuffed me to this mother fucking bed.

"Bitch are you crazy?" I'm guessing she was because she started pacing walking back and forth talking to herself and me at the same damn time. When I saw the spit flying from her mouth I knew I had fucked up.

"All the fuck he had to do was listen to me. Why the fuck wouldn't you listen to me? She thinks she can come back in and take what's mine. I got a trick for her ass. Hell, I got a trick for you too if you want to play with me. You are mine and you are never leaving me. I fought for you. Do you hear me. She let you go, but I didn't." Next thing you know, this bitch picked up the piss bucket and started beating me with it. "I always give my all and they still leave." She hit me 3 more times. The whole time I was trying to dodge the spit that was flying out of her mouth. If her mouth got this wet when she was giving head she would do good. *Bam. Bam. Bam.* I guess she noticed I wasn't paying attention and started beating me more. In the midst of her rant, she said something that caught my attention. She said the bitch let you go. Me and Tank had some type of dealings. *Bam.* She hit me again before walking out of the room. This bitch was stray jacket crazy and when I get out of this she is going to see she fucked with the wrong nigga.

5- THREE PEAT

"Fucking right ho, I might go crazy on these niggas I don't give a mother fuck. Run up in a nigga house and shoot his grandmother up. What. I don't give a mother fuck get your baby kidnapped and your baby mother fucked." Lil Wayne

TANK...

I was trying my best to stay strong for Nik, but being in this hospital was breaking me down. I was just here and was told my husband was cremated. There was no fucking way that I wanted to be in here again, but my brother and my bitch needed me. We were waiting on the doctor to come talk to us when Gangsta walked in.

"Sis, what are they saying?"

"We are waiting on the doctor to come talk to us. He is in surgery right now."

"My nigga better pull through it. I can't lose anybody else. I'm working on something though. I'm going to keep you posted, but when I leave here I will let you know if I have a destination on that nigga Sin. I know everybody wants a piece of him, so I won't do it until you all get there."

"I don't know Gangsta. I may have to let you do that shit on your own. I saw how your brother did my friend and you are worse than he is. I don't think I can stomach the kind of death you are going to bring." Laughing at me.

"I know your tough ass ain't afraid of a lil blood. Not tough ass Tank." I slapped him on the arm and looked up because the doctor was approaching us. I wrapped my arms around Nik just in case she needed me.

"He is going to pull through. He is just fine. The bullet that went through his neck went straight through. It was a flesh wound. The shots to his chest were more critical, but we removed both bullets and he is doing fine. You all can go back and see him." The doctor stated and walked off. I hugged Nik because I was happy for her, but in the back of my mind I was wondering why they couldn't do it for Suave. We all headed to the back knowing damn well it was only supposed to be 2 at a time.

"Damn nigga you look like shit. Look like you need a biscuit." Gangsta joked with Smalls.

"Nigga, the mother fucker that shot me probably ate it. He was big as shit and wanted to fight."

"How did you get shot then?" I asked, I was confused.

"I upped my piece on the big mother fucker and next thing you know we were in a full shoot out. Lil Goon decided he wanted to be Tony Montana and ran his little ass back out there. I went to grab him and some nigga came out the house and lit me up. I got his ass though. He up there arguing with Jesus trying to get in them gates." We all laughed, but Nik didn't find the shit funny. She walked up to Lil Goon and started swinging on his ass.

"Smalls get your girl nigga." Goon yelled while trying to dodge the hits.

"Nik, you better keep a gun on you. Your ass really can't fight bae." I don't know why Smalls said that because she walked up to him and slapped him like 3 times.

"I'm glad you think this funny. I almost lost you and your funky ass in here making jokes." She finally calmed down and sat on the bed with him. You can tell everybody wanted to laugh, but we didn't want to piss her off again.

"I called Suave phone and somebody answered." I blurted out.

"Sis, did you take that urn out my house like I asked you? I'm not playing with your ass. That shit better be gone when I get there." Smalls said serious as hell.

"I'm serious I showed it to Nik. Somebody has his phone. They answered it."

"Sis, go see that officer and see if he can track the location of it. If Sin has it then we know where he is." Gangsta advised me. I don't know why I didn't think of that. Probably because I wanted it to be Suave on the other end of the phone.

"I will go see him when I leave from here."

"Now, somebody go get me some food." Smalls ass was always talking about food. We continued to joke and have a good time. I was grateful for some good news for once and we may have a lead on Sin.

PARADISE...

I paced back and forth in the room that I was being held in. It was definitely an upgrade from the warehouse. Whoever lived here had money, but I was still being held against my will. There was a bathroom and clothes in the closet, so I decided to wash my ass. It felt good to finally have water running over my body and not them damn wet wipes Sin gave me. I stood in there about an hour. I wanted the scent of him off me. The more I washed the more I could smell him. As soon as I got dressed I heard the door unlocking. I braced myself so that I could attack whoever came through the door. I needed to get home to G. I had to get out of here. The door swung open and my mouth fell open in astonishment. I ran to him and jumped in his arms.

"Papa. How did you find me? I am so glad to see you. Get the men together we have to go find Sincere and kill him."

"Slow down baby girl. One thing at a time. I found you because I have been watching you for a while. I knew that low life was going to fuck up and I would be able to bring you home."

"Wait. You have been watching me the whole time and you allowed me to stay chained up in that warehouse? Are you fucking serious. Why papa?" Tears were now coming down my face. This was the first time I cried in front of my father in 15 years. He did not tolerate weakness.

"Everything I did was to protect you. If I had let you go then you would have went back to him. I couldn't allow that. When you escaped I had to grab you. As far as Sin goes. We know exactly where he is."

"Then let's go get him. He did very bad things to me papa. He hurt me badly."

"We are not going to get him Paradise." I had the dumbest look on my face. Did he not hear what I just said?

"Why aren't we going to get him?"

"Because I am already here." Sin walked into the bedroom. My sadness turned to anger and I ran towards him ready to tear him apart with my bare hands. My papa intervened and held me.

"You were working with him the whole time?" I looked to my papa for answers.

"No. I told you I was watching you. I didn't realize Sin had kidnapped you for about a month. I approached him and we united to take down a common enemy."

"Gangsta." I said in disbelief.

"Yes, baby your boyfriend is beneath this family and I don't need you going back complicating things. You are now where you belong, but until he is handled you will remain locked in this room. There are bars on your window and the door is pad locked from the other side. Sit down and relax. He will be here soon and I promise to let you reunite before I kill him. Dinner will be up shortly. Oh, and Paradise, don't let me catch you crying again. " He walked out and I tried to attack him from behind. His security detail dragged my ass right back in the room. After they locked the door I tried to think of a plan. I had to figure out a way to warn G. After thinking of every possible outcome, I cried. At the end of this, I would have to go to war with my father. That was a war I wasn't sure I would be able to fight.

GANGSTA...

I was supposed to meet up with Sinay at 8 tonight for our date, but I decided to swing by earlier. I had a surprise for her. Pulling up to her house I got out of my car and walked up to the door. Waiting on her to open it, I felt an excitement I haven't felt in a long time. She opened the door looking shocked.

"Gangsta, what are you doing here? We weren't supposed to meet until later. I still have my daughter."

"It's ok. I have a surprise for you and her, so I came earlier. It's not a problem is it? I can come back?"

"No, it's fine. You can come in." walking in I noticed her daughter sitting on the floor playing with her baby dolls. She was adorable. I could see why Paradise wanted children, but it would be just my luck my baby came out ugly as fuck with snot always running down her nose begging for candy and shit.

"Hey princess. How are you? My name is Kenneth, what's yours?"

"Hi, my name is Harem. Are you my mommy's friend?"

"Yes, and I was hoping I could be your friend too." She looked up at me and smiled. I looked over at Sinay and it was almost as if she didn't know what to say to me.

"Do you want something to drink?" I nodded my head at her and she went in the kitchen. I hurried up and set up my surprise for her. I wanted the shock factor. It took her about 5 minutes to come back out with a half of cup of Kool Aid, but it was all good because it gave me time to make sure I was done with the surprise.

"G, what the fuck are you doing?" I had my gun raised at her and her daughter was tied up to the chair.

"We are playing a game. Me and Harem decided to play cops and robbers. Now come sit down." Looking horrified she came and sat next to her daughter. I tied her up and then decided to explain.

"Bitch if you thought for one second pussy could cloud my judgment you had me fucked up. Me killing your mother was a message to Sin. There was no way he didn't know I killed her. Then you just happened to be in the hood. You gotta be quicker than that Sinay. I know you are probably mad at your brother right now, but it didn't matter. I was coming to kill you next anyway."

"Please don't. I am someone's mother. She is right here. Are you really going to kill me in front of my daughter?"

"Actually, I'm not. What kind of monster do you take me for?" She looked relieved. I pulled a bottle out of my pocket and walked towards Harem.

"Hey pretty girl, I want you to taste my magic potion. I bet you it can put you to sleep for 10 minutes."

"No it can't. Let me see." She said excitedly.

"G, please. Don't hurt her."

"Didn't you just hear me say it will put her to sleep for 10 minutes." I poured the liquid down Harem's throat. I made sure to give her a high dose. I needed it to work right away. I watched her until her head dropped. Looking back at Sinay, I moved forward with my plan.

"Now, I am going to ask you the same thing I asked your mom. Where is your brother?"

"I swear to you G, he didn't tell us where he was. He pops up over here or calls me from some burner phone. I don't know where he is. Please listen to me, I don't know."

"Guess that's fucked up for you. There is another way to save your life Sinay. If you can make me nut, I will let you live." I could see her think it over and she agreed.

"Okay, we have to hurry before my daughter wakes back up." I let her loose and kept my gun pointed at her the entire time. She quickly dropped to her knees and pulled my dick out. I could tell she really wanted to live because this bitch went to work on my meat. Each time she went down she deep throated me. Took in all 10 inches like a pro. Using her hands to create a circular motion while she sucked that shit was making me brick hard. She almost made me nut in 2 minutes. I had to gather myself. Once she started moaning while she was sucking me, the shit made me moan. My legs were shaking and my knees were getting weak. All you heard were moans and slurps. She sucked the pre cum from my tip and spit it back on my dick and kept sucking. When she slid my balls in her mouth at the same time, I was done.

"You like that don't you baby?" The bitch was asking questions, but I was trying to concentrate on holding my nut. I knew I couldn't stay in this position long or it was over for me.

"Turn around. I want to get inside of you." She obliged and I slid straight in that monkey. I couldn't believe she was so wet. Grabbing her by her ass cheeks, I did what I do best. I tore that ass up. No bitch would go see Jesus thinking she had one upped me before she left. Slamming into her, I knew it was hurting. But she was so determined to make me nut she started throwing that ass back. Her ass cheeks were jiggling with each stroke. Pulling her ass cheeks apart, I watched as I dug in and out of her. I loved how my dick looked going in and out of some pussy no matter what the situation was. I wasn't selfish, so I decided to let her get one last nut. Reaching my hand to the front of her, I massaged her clit as I slammed my dick in her. She was no longer just trying to get me to nut, she was all into it. I felt her muscles gripping on my dick and that shit drove me crazy. Once I felt her bust, I was relieved because I could finally let mine go.

"Fuck baby, I'm about to cum." She gripped her muscles against my dick again and I nutted instantly. All these years and this pussy was exactly how I imagined it. I stood up and put my meat back in my draws. "Damn, I knew you had some good pussy." She stood up looking satisfied.

"How long will it be before Harem wakes up?"

"Aww I lied. Your mama up there babysitting her until you get there." Her mouth fell open from shock.

"Oh my God I can't believe you killed my baby." I could tell she wanted to try something, so I raised my gun back up.

"You don't want to do anything stupid."

"I thought you said if I can make you nut you will let me live."

"Oh I lied about that too. Suave always told me, a bitch that can squeeze your dick with her pussy is the devil. It's only room for one Lucifer in this city." I pulled the trigger. I made a mistake and left my gas can, so I had to do something creative to send Sin a message.

SIN...

I was talking with Louis when my phone rang. I told her to call me when they went on their date and that wasn't until 8, so I ignored the call. She wouldn't stop calling so I answered.

"What's up sis. I'm handling some business getting it ready for tonight."

"Gangsta is here now. He just got here said he has a surprise for me and the baby and wants to kick it now."

"Good, that mean you got the nigga where you want him. I can gather up the team and be there in an hour. Just don't act like you gone fuck him until I text you. That will mean I'm about 5 minutes away."

"You sure about this? Are you really going to kill him? He was like our brother."

"I'm not about to go through this with you again. The nigga is in the next room. I can't have him over hearing this conversation. Get your shit together and go in there and make that nigga want you." I hung up because she was starting to piss me off. Bitch gone fuck up our plan. This was the closest we have come to finding his ass I wasn't about to let her ruin that for me. She should be just as pissed as I was. He killed our fucking mama. She better be lucky I didn't ask her ass to suck his dick. I finished doing what I was doing and told the team to get ready. We were about to take down the devil. They said if you kill the head the body will fall. I already got rid of Suave and now I was finally about to take out his bitch ass brother.

I texted Sinay when were about to pull up. I gave her 10 minutes instead of 5 to make sure the nigga was good and relaxed. When we pulled up I didn't see G's car. His scary ass must have hidden it. Me, Louis, and 5 other niggas surrounded the house. I looked at Louis and he signaled for me to go in. Walking in the door, I immediately started throwing up.

"Looks like you have underestimated your opponent. Your friend has come and gone." I wanted to slap the shit out of him. He didn't have an ounce of remorse. My sister and niece's head was hanging from the chandelier and the rest of their body was gone. This sick ass nigga killed my fucking niece. This is the first time G has killed a kid. He usually doesn't kill innocent bystanders. Guilt ran all through me. My whole family was dead because of my greed. I did this, but there was no turning back now. I was going to kill Gangsta if it was the last thing I did on this earth. I stood there looking at my people, what was left of them and started crying. I don't think the tears made it all the way down my face before I felt the blow. *BOOM.*

"Crying is for the weak. I don't tolerate weak men on my team. They are gone. Pull yourself together immediately. You have 5 minutes to make peace with your decision and come outside. I don't want to see a trace of sadness on your face when you walk out the door." I can't believe this nigga just smacked me with his gun. I wanted to knock his old ass out, but his security looked at me like they dared me to try it. I was starting to regret my decision to cross Gangsta. This nigga doesn't play fair and I no longer had any pieces to play. Louis was not going to allow me to kill Paradise and I was now being ran by someone else. I wiped the tears from my eyes and fixed my face. It was too late for them. I had to move forward and deal with it.

HARPER...

I could feel myself falling apart. This is not how this was supposed to go. I needed Kendyl on my side and I now had the leverage to do so. I didn't mean to slip up and say so much about Tank, but I still had the upper hand. He doesn't know how he knows her. Only what I told him. I was about to fix this and move on with my life with my man. Unlocking the door, I walked in the room and he looked pissed. I could tell he wasn't used to being treated like this. I sat his tray of food down and hoped we could have a civilized conversation.

"I know you are pissed off, but I need for you to understand. I can't lose you. I may be pregnant and I'm going to need you to be a great father and be here for the baby."

"Bitch you done lost your mind. You want me to stay here with your crazy ass. You got me fucked up." Dead set on showing him that Tank was not the woman for him, I pulled the proof out of my pocket and put it up to his face.

"I told you she was not yours. You are my husband. She belongs to another man. You are breaking up our relationship over someone who is not even thinking about you." He looked at the picture and started laughing.

"Your dumb ass plan done fell apart like them ugly ass shoes of yours. The nigga in the picture is my brother. I knew something was wrong with your story. I don't think you have any idea who the fuck you are messing with. If you let me go now I promise not to kill you." Standing up I stood over him and punched his ass in the mouth. The madder I got the more I hit him.

"You ungrateful, selfish, hood rat. I saved your fucking life and that little tramp of yours was nowhere in sight. Nobody showed up for you. I was there willing you back to life. Me! Nobody else. You don't want me? Then you no longer want my help." I grabbed his tray of food and flung it to the floor. I was done playing games with him. Whether it was voluntary or involuntary, he was going to stay right here and be my man. I gave him one last look and he licked the blood from his lips and spoke.

"Bitch when I get loose, I promise you are going to die a slow painful death." I walked out and closed the door. Rubbing my stomach, I prayed I was pregnant. Then he would stay. He would love me then. I just needed to be pregnant.

GANGSTA...

I had just picked up Journey when Smalls asked me to come grab him from the hospital. It seems like every time we try to hook up lately, something else comes up. He was being released and nobody else was answering their phone.

I couldn't leave my nigga out there like that, so I agreed. I can tell she was mad, but this time I tried to smooth it over. I missed her and I needed some of that good pussy tonight.

"Baby I promise it won't take that long. All we are doing is picking him up and dropping him off."

"That's not the point. As of late, you continuously put me off for someone else. Everybody comes before me. I had a special night for us planned and on top of that I'm horny.

"That's what your problem is huh. You miss daddy's dick? Don't worry, I promise I'm all yours after we drop him off. Where are we going anyway?"

"I found this beautiful bed and breakfast on the out skirts of town. It is amazing. I just thought after everything that happened, you deserved a night away from it all."

"And I appreciate that girl. I got you and I can't wait to see it." We pulled up to the hospital and I couldn't wait to drop Smalls ass off. Sinay's pussy was good as fuck, but it didn't have shit on Journey's. That squirting shit had a nigga addicted. Don't get me wrong, Paradise is still the best I ever had, but that squirting shit had a nigga gone. My dick was hard thinking about it. Smalls was being wheeled out to the car. The nurse helped him in and I drove off.

"Damn nigga, I barely closed the door. Fuck is wrong with you."

"Nigga I got somewhere to be and you interrupted that."

"Niggas get pussy everyday B." This nigga was saying it like Rico off Paid in Full. He was trying to be funny, but I didn't want him messing up my pussy tonight.

"Hey slow that shit down. You see my girl in the car."

"Nigga you tripping. Last I checked, I got shot up from being out here in these streets looking for your girl. Now let me know, if this is your girl who the fuck I get shot for?"

"Aight nigga chill out. I get your point. Let me hurry up and drop your ass off." I looked over at Journey and she was pissed.

"If I don't get no pussy tonight, I'm coming back to your crib and I'm going to slap your ass with Suave's ashes. Dumb ass nigga, because your dick don't work, you gone fuck up my shit." He laughed, but I was dead ass serious. I got to that nigga house and I damn near dragged him up the stairs.

"Damn nigga, you gone kill me over some pussy?" He had damn near fell.

"I gotta go do damage control. My dick harder than a nigga on C block 4 and you playing with me. Move shit."

He laughed as I ran back down the stairs. Jumping in the car I tried to salvage our night.

"You have to understand, that's their sister. They don't approve of us, but it's not up to them. I want to be with you, so I am here. Okay?"

"It's okay baby, I understand. Let's just get to our spot and enjoy our night." That's what the fuck I'm talking about. I'm glad she understood. I just hope she would be this understanding when I found Paradise and I had to dump her ass. My mission never changed. I just needed her to get over the loneliness. I drove to our destination with a lot on my mind.

6- IT WOULD BE YOU

"Your shoes can't be filled, they can not fill your heels. My truth is in you, there is nothing that's real as our love. I'll be just fine as long as you're by my side... If I could have anything, I put that on everything that it would be you. I just want you." Trey Songs

TANK...

I already told the fellas what my plan was, but Smalls was in the hospital, Gangsta had a lead, and my bitches couldn't go with me today. Everybody told me we would handle it later on tonight, but I didn't give a fuck. I was going to figure out who the fuck had my man phone. I wasn't going to go busting in on no rah rah shit. I would sit outside and see who would go in and out of the location. I had already went to Suave's cop friend and he tracked it to the last location when the phone was on. Of course, the location was Indiana. Once this was over I promise a mother fucker couldn't pay me to take my ass across that bridge. Driving to the location I parked down from the house a little bit. Sitting there I wondered who the fuck lived in this big ass house. It was damn near the size of ours and we had millions. It was in a white upscale neighborhood. I was starting to think somebody may have found his phone, when I saw someone walking out the door. What the fuck. It was the doctor that told me Suave was dead. What would she be doing with his phone. If it was in his property, why didn't she give it to me. This shit wasn't making sense. I watched her jump in her car and leave. I waited about 15 minutes to make sure that she wasn't coming back. I got out of my car and creeped up to the house. She must have been pissed when she left because she left the door unlocked. I walked slowly through the big ass house, not knowing what I was looking for. It looked like she lived here alone. It was very cold and not in a temperature kind of way. It was like there was no love in this house. No pictures or anything. I walked to the back of the house and there was a door. I tried it, but it was locked. I learned from movies whenever you saw a locked door that meant the person was crazy as shit. I reached in my pocket and pulled out my silencer. Twisting it on I looked around to see if I could see inside the room. Once I saw I couldn't I walked off to go look through the rest of the house.

"I swear to God I'm going to kill this bitch." I know it was through a locked door, but I would know Suave's voice if he was under water. If I called anybody they would say I was crazy and losing my mind. Was I two thoughts away from being admitted? Why would the doctor have Suave? The lock on the door was a padlock, I knew I couldn't shoot it off. I decided to hide in the closet across from it until she came home. I hope she would come unlock the door. If she didn't I would have to make her.

After being in the closet for over an hour, I was about to come out and find something in the house to knock that mother fucker off the hinges when I heard her come in the door. I cracked the closet just enough so I could see her when she came this way. I could hear her walking down the hall and my heart was racing. I heard the door unlock and she went in the room. Easing out the closet I walked up to the now open door to see if I could hear his voice again. She was talking.

"I had time to calm down and I want to apologize. We both were angry and said somethings we shouldn't have. This is not good for the baby. We need to figure out a way to get back to us." Baby!! I know the fuck he didn't get this bitch pregnant. This couldn't be Suave. There is no way he would cheat on me.

"Bitch you are delusional. I meant every fucking word I said. When I get out of this shit I am going to kill you dead. You psychotic, dry, old ass bitch." *SLAP*... It was definitely Suave and she had just slapped the shit out of him.

"You disrespectful mother fucker. Quit fooling yourself. You are not going to kill me."

"I am." She turned around and her face almost hit the floor when she saw me.

"What are you doing in my house? Get the fuck out now!" She acted like she still had the authority.

"Tank?" He didn't say it like he knew it was me. It was like he was asking a question. I looked at him and he was handcuffed to what looked like a hospital bed.

"The one and fucking only."

"Whoever you are, get out of my house before I call the police." I didn't even feel like going back and forth. *Pow. Pow. Pow.* I shot the bitch 3 times in the chest. I walked up to her and snatched the keys from around her neck. I didn't know how to feel about Suave at this moment, but I uncuffed him. What the fuck did this nigga have on? I had so many questions, but first I had to make sure this bitch wouldn't wake up and stab our ass.

"Get her on the bed now." He picked her up, but I could tell he was grunting and in pain. I cuffed her and now I would get my answers.

"What the fuck is going on Suave? Why the fuck don't you know who I am and why is she talking about a damn baby?" He walked up to me and kissed me so passionately my knees buckled.

"I know exactly who you are baby. The shit is so confusing, but I will try to explain it to you the best way I can. When I woke up, I was here. I had no idea who this person was or why she had me. She kept telling me that she was my wife and that I was shot in a robbery attempt. I told her about you and my life and she told me I was dreaming. She pulled up all this research telling me that my condition was common for coma patients. I didn't know who I was or what to believe, but I felt you in my soul. She would cry and get upset because she said I didn't remember my wife, but I remembered my wife from a dream. I kept asking questions and she took me to a psychiatrist at the hospital and everything that Harper had told me this doctor said the same thing, but when we were leaving I saw you. I guess she knew I was going to leave and she handcuffed me to this damn bed. Told me she was about to check my vitals." He turned from me and punched her so hard in the face her nose broke. I can't believe this crazy bitch was just gone take her a man. He walked over to a table and started grabbing utensils.

"Suave, are you about to pull a Gangsta?"

"You can wait outside if you don't want to see this. I told her she was going to die a slow, painful death and I always keep my promises." He didn't even look up at me as he prepared to torture her. I didn't like shit like this, but the pain she caused me made me want to stay. I walked over to where he was grabbing all kinds of shit and I grabbed what looked like a knife.

"Tank what the fuck are you doing?" Suave knew that this type of killing wasn't my thing.

"This bitch said she was pregnant and after reading all of Mz. Lady P books I'm not taking no chances. All them mother fuckers come back to life and I'll be damned if a nappy head, stuck up, crazy ass baby show up on my door step."

"I don't know who Lady P is, but both of yall are crazy." He laughed.

"That's boss lady and fuck yea she is crazy." Raising the knife, I stabbed her ass in the stomach like 10 times. I needed to make sure that if it was a possibility of a baby, it was gone. I don't raise other women raggedy ass kids. Satisfied that I made sure I stabbed any sperm that could have been spinning around in that shit, I moved out the way to let him do his thing so we could get the fuck out of dodge. As soon as he started, I regretted not leaving. The first thing he did was cut around her eyeballs with a scalpel. If the bitch wasn't dead before then, I'm sure she was now from the pain. Sliding the scalpel under her eyeballs, he popped them bitches out like he was about to eat some damn crab legs. I felt the vomit rising in my throat. Trying to stand firm and be there for my man, I pushed it back down. When that nigga started outlining her face with the scalpel I had to ask what he was about to do.

"Bae, are you about to take her face off?"

"Just the skin, not the whole thing baby." He laughed like that made it better.

Gangsta's Paradise 2: How Deep Is Your Love — Latoya Nicole

"Yeah, I'm going to wait outside." Walking out I could hear him laughing at me. I thanked God everyday he forgave me for robbing him, because that could have been me on that table. They always call Gangsta the devil, but when Suave is pissed, he is just as bad. Them niggas needed a hug or something. I walked around the bitch house just to try and understand her. Trying to get a clue of what she was like, I walked in her closet. How in the fuck this nigga fell for her lies is beyond me. The only thing in this bitch closet was Sketchers and Easy Spirits. I died laughing at the thought of him out in public with her. Everything about this bitch was dull and boring. No wonder she had to take a man, nobody in their right mind would voluntarily endure this shit. I was starting to get creeped out and I just wanted to get the fuck from out of this hoe house. Walking in the kitchen I walked over to the gas line and pulled it a loose. Not wanting it to blow before I was ready, I eased out of the kitchen trying not to bump anything. Walking back in the room where my baby was doing his thing, I made the mistake of looking on the table. I immediately threw up. This nigga had all kinds of parts just lying there. Eyeballs, her face, fingers, and some other shit I don't even know what it was.

"Baby that's enough, it's time to go home, let's go." The nigga must have been in a trance, because he didn't hear shit I said he just kept working. I walked over to him and grabbed his hand and pulled him away. "Baby, it's over. We can go home now. Let's get out of here." He allowed me to lead him out of the house. He was about to walk out of the gate when he saw me walking around the side of the house.

"What are you doing Tank?" He was looking confused.

"Cleaning up behind ourselves." I raised my gun and shot into the kitchen. I didn't stop until I saw the flames. Grabbing his hand, I led him to my car and we went home.

SUAVE...

Seeing Tank walk through that door brought a feeling over me I had never felt. I have never been in a situation where I needed someone to save me and the one time I was, my better half found me. I don't even know how she ended up here, but I was grateful that she did. That's how I know she was my soul mate. Usually, I would be pissed if she did some shit like this. Hell, I told her she couldn't even carry her gun anymore, but on today I was happy she didn't listen. Driving back to the house, I didn't even know what to say. I deliberately left out that I slept with Harper. That was a fight I didn't want to have. It was not needed. I didn't want her and now the bitch was gone. I almost forgot the reason I was shot in the first place.

"Have you guys found Paradise and Sin?"

"Nope, and Smalls just got shot up while he was looking for him." I knew he had to be okay because of how she said it.

"This nigga is really starting to piss me off. I can't wait to get my hands on his ass. How did you find me?"

"Well, me and Smalls had the address that I gave you when you said it was nothing. He said it was no way that you didn't go check it out. We went there and it was blood everywhere. I saw pill bottles and it said Sin name. I told you that nigga was in on it." She side-eyed me and I couldn't do shit but take it because she was right. "Then we tracked your car and it was in Indiana. I got tired of sitting around doing nothing, so me and the girls went to every hospital and jail in Indiana. The last one I went to told me you were admitted. We got upstairs and that bitch you was just with told me you died the night before and gave me some ashes and said they cremated you. Everybody thought I was crazy because I kept saying I didn't believe you was dead. I kept calling your phone and the bitch made a mistake and answered. I had the officer track your phone and I snuck off and came to see who had it." She looked at me nervously.

"Normally, I would be pissed. You are pregnant and you shouldn't have done something like this on your own, but you followed your heart and it led you to me. I can't be mad at that. Thank you Lashay." I leaned over and kissed her. We finally pulled up to the house and I knew this was going to freak everybody out. I allowed Tank to go in first. Smalls and Nik were sitting in the front room.

"Hey yall. I brought somebody here to see you. He said he missed yall." Tank said leaving them guessing. I walked in the door and Smalls jumped up and pulled his gun on me. That damn sure wasn't the response I was looking for.

"Sis, I told your ass I don't play that ghost shit. Now you got 10 seconds to tell me what the fuck is going on before I start airing Casper ass out." He was dead ass serious too.

"Brother, it's not a ghost. It's really him. Some crazy bitch was holding him hostage." Tank explained.

"Now get that fucking gun out of my face before I beat your ass." I don't care how weird this was, I didn't play that shit.

"Well if you are really Suave, then who the fuck is this?" He walked over to an urn and picked it up.

"Man, I have no idea." He walked to the door and threw the ashes out.

"You mean to tell me, it's a nigga I don't know been walking around here looking at my balls and shit?" Smalls screamed.

"Nigga what are you talking about?"

"Man nothing, but what the fuck you got on. Nigga get shot and come back as Carlton. Them some ugly ass loafers." I couldn't do shit, but laugh at his crazy ass.

"Where the fuck is G?"

"He on a date or some shit. I don't know that nigga been tripping, but hey nigga for real what you got on?" I shook my head because this nigga wasn't going to stop.

"Baby, speaking of Gangsta. That nigga busted my lip. We made up, but he had my shit on swoll for days." Smalls started laughing so hard he had to grab his wound.

"What the fuck is funny nigga. I'm going to beat that nigga ass."

"Because I knew she was gone tell on his ass. I told him you were going to fuck him up, but we about to leave yall alone. I know yall got some making up to do. Just don't be too loud I don't want to hear that shit." Him and Nik walked to the room. Her big pregnant ass was practically carrying him. I looked over at my baby and she never looked more beautiful. I picked her up around my waist and carried her to our room. Walking into the bathroom I put her down and removed her clothes. I turned on the shower and removed mine as well. She grabbed the loofah and soaped it up. Gently, she began washing me up. The soap burned against my wounds, but my baby took her time cleaning me. It felt way different from Harper's touch. Just looking at her made my dick hard. I leaned down and kissed her. When I did, tears started flowing down her face. I wiped them away and kissed her more passionately this time. I poured my soul into her with my kiss.

"Don't cry baby, I am here. I told you, I will always come back to you." Grabbing her face to me I started slowly licking her neck. Making my way down her body, I stopped at her nipples. Taking each one into my mouth I sucked them softly, but with urgency. I kept going down until I found my way to her soft spot. Using my tongue to find her clit, I slid my tongue up and down until I could taste her juices. Sucking her clit until I felt it swell, I made love to it with my tongue for about 30 minutes. She was about to cum for the 3rd time when I stopped. I stood up and turned her around. Sliding my dick inside of her, I moaned out in ecstasy. I know I was probably sounding like a bitch, but there was no better feeling in this world. Her pussy fit me like a glove. No matter how wet she got, her pussy was always tight. Sliding in and out of her, I felt my dick swell up. I knew there was nothing I could do about this first nut. It was coming whether I wanted it to or not. I didn't fight it. I shot that shit up to her throat. Stepping out the shower. I grabbed a towel and dried her off. Once we got in the bed, I told her to lay down on her stomach. I grabbed some oil off the dresser and poured it on her body. Massaging every part of her I made my way back up to her ass. It was a beautiful site. I kept spreading her cheeks apart as I caressed them. I couldn't take it anymore. I was back hard. I lifted her ass up to me and slid my dick up and down her slit. Her moans started driving me crazy. I wanted to make love to her, but my dick was craving her too bad. Once I slid it in, my pace picked up immediately. I didn't think it through when I poured all that damn oil on her because I couldn't get a good grip. I leaned forward and grabbed her breast for leverage. That was better. Slamming my dick inside her, she went crazy. The only sounds you could hear was our moans and my balls slapping against her ass.

"Tell me you love me." I whispered.

"I love you baby." Her voice made my dick go brick. I pulled her up until she was on all 4's and went to work. Pushing all 11 inches inside of her, I felt her body start to shake. I pulled out and ate her pussy from the back. Sucking her clit until she came all in my mouth.

"Fuck baby, I missed you Suave. Please don't ever leave me. Fuck, don't stop baby. Don't stop." I couldn't respond because my mouth was full. After I caught all of her juices, her body was shaking out of control., but I stood back up and slammed my dick right back inside of her. Slapping her ass with each stroke, I could feel my nut about to rise. If she wasn't already pregnant she would have definitely been tonight. My body started shaking and I had an orgasm like never before. My legs went numb and I couldn't do anything, but collapse. My eyes started to close right away. I was damn near sleep when Tank spoke up.

"Baby, can we go home now?" She said just above a whisper.

"You know we can't do that. We can't leave until we find Paradise and kill Sin. I will not leave until that mother fucker is dead." She got really quiet and then she spoke again.

"I want to be there when it is done. We will leave directly after. Anybody that don't get to tell us good bye can do it over face time." I knew that was hard for her, but I loved her for understanding.

"Agreed." Now let me get some sleep. I have to call G in the morning. It's time to wrap this shit up." 2 minutes later I was out like a light.

7- WRONG SIDE OF A LOVE SONG

"And you got me singing why, why you wanna make me cry? I'll be thinking bout you, got me dreaming bout you every single day and night. And I don't wanna be without you, cause I could hardly breathe without you. This is what it feels to be the one who's standing left behind. How did I become the wrong side of a love song?" Melonie Fiona

PARADISE...

I was sitting in my room reading. I had just finished with *Trenae's You gon pay me with tears 2* and I downloaded my next book to read by *Aj Davidson Cherished by a Boss.* Changing positions because my arm was falling asleep, my room door unlocked. I had been stuck in here all day and nobody had come to check on me so I decided to read books. It felt good to read about somebody else's drama other than my own. When I saw my father, I looked back down and continued to read. I had no words for him. He had betrayed me and for what? To hurt a man he didn't even know. I was pissed at G, but he didn't deserve this. I know all of it was my fault and I just had to figure out a way to warn him. I had to get out of this room.

"I see you still aren't talking to me?" I didn't look up at him, so he kept talking. "Listen, I know you may not agree with my methods, but you will understand them some day. That man is not good for you."

"How do you know that papa? You don't even know him and was allowing me to get kidnapped and raped what's best for me? You are a fucking joke. Get the fuck out of my face."

"I don't give a fuck how mad you are at me, YOU WILL RESPECT ME. Now get yourself together and come downstairs. I have something to show you and hurry up before I forget you are my daughter." I didn't care about nothing else he said. I was getting out of this room. As soon as I got downstairs I would make a run for it. Or so I thought. I walked out of the room and my papa's security was waiting on me with guns drawn. I could have cried. Feeling defeated I walked downstairs. When I walked in the den it was a woman there that I never seen before.

"Who the fuck are you?" She just looked at me. I think she was more shocked than I was.

"Paradise, I am not going to tell you again about your disrespect. Before I introduce you two, it's somebody else I want you to see." All of us went through his secret door and ended up in another room. I looked up and I almost passed out.

"Gangsta!!! Oh my God baby." I tried to run to him, but I was stopped.

"Now you know that is not about to happen. Besides, I think that would be disrespectful to his baby mother." I looked at my father like he had lost his mind, but when I looked at G, I could see the sadness form in his eyes. "Paradise, this is Journey your sister." Me and Gangsta both looked up and mirrored the same look.

"What the fuck. I don't have a sister. I'm an only child." I could tell that Journey didn't know this bit of news either.

"Wait, so you had me approach and seduce this man knowing he was my sister's boyfriend?" She looked horrified.

"Yes, and it worked. Jimmy will pay you, and your services are no longer needed. You can leave." My papa instructed.

"Hold the fuck on." G was livid. "How much did you get paid? I want to know how much your life is worth. I promise you bitch, you will die. I hope it was worth it."

"Settle down Kenneth. You will not be getting out of here. You will die in this house. I'm sure 500k was a sufficient payment." My papa said in a matter of fact tone.

"Was losing you daughter worth 500k? You sent in my so called sister to fuck my man and you think we are going to live happily ever after?" I turned to face the bitch that fucked my man. "Journey, even if G don't get out of this, I will and I am going to kill you." I looked at G "This is the bitch you chose to get pregnant? But I wasn't good enough. Fuck everybody in this room." I got ready to storm out, but my father stopped me.

"Let's not climb on that high horse so fast. Sin come here." Gangsta head turned so fast and that sadness was now gone. You can see pure murder in his eyes. "Now Paradise can stand here and condemn you for your affair with Journey, but did she tell you she had an affair with Sincere? It was her idea to stage the fake kidnapping, but when she tried to back out Sin held her for real." The look on Gangsta's face shattered my soul. I never had any intentions on telling him of my affair with Sin. I felt like pure dog shit standing in that room.

"G, I'm sorry. I was unhappy and just trying to get you to love me." The look on his face told me that he didn't give a shit about my apology.

"You and that nigga better hope Aids kill you first, because when I get out of here I'm going to kill everybody." He spat at me.

"AIDS!!!" Everybody said at the same time.

"He didn't tell you he is dying slow anyway? Now you and him can go together."

"I promise we used a condom every time. I promise. Even when I gave him head. He insisted on it."

"Ain't that sweet. The fairy has a fucking conscience. I'm surprised he fucked you. I didn't know you was his type since he likes getting fucked in the ass." I knew it was true because I witnessed it firsthand, the night he shot Suave. Sin looked embarrassed as fuck. He walked over to G and punched him in the face.

"You, I will give this shit to. Shut the fuck up before I fuck you and your ass die slow with me." Sin screamed at G.

"Hold on, there won't be any gay torture going on in here. I don't allow that gay shit under my roof. For the record, being gay is a weakness. I told you earlier I couldn't have weak men on my crew. You can leave with Journey. I will compensate you for your services as well. Now I'm glad we are all caught up, but I have business to attend to. Jimmy, pay these two and show them out. Everybody else, take Paradise back up to her room. Gangsta, you hold tight. I have something special planned for you." With that he walked out leaving us all there to think about everything that was said. On my way back to my room, my heart ached for Gangsta. He had just been betrayed by everybody in that room. I can't even imagine how he felt. How did it all come down to this?

GANGSTA...

I couldn't wait to get away from Smalls ass. My dick was hard as hell and I needed to release in the worse way. Journey was steady smirking at me and shit, rubbing my meat through my pants. I was about to pull over and handle her ass on the highway if she didn't stop. We pulled up to this secluded ass mansion and I must say it was nice as fuck. Only a chick would find some shit like this. A nigga would have taken her straight to motel 6. Laughing at my own joke I parked my car and got out. She grabbed my hand and walked me towards the door. When it opened, we walked in and the butler told us the host would be with us momentarily. Standing there looking around the mansion, I thought to myself I had never seen a hotel that looked like this. It only took me about 2 minutes to start getting that feeling that some shit wasn't right. Reaching in my waistband, I realized I left my gun in the car.

"I'll be right back, I left something." It's not that I thought Journey would play me, but something felt off and my brother always told me to trust my instincts. Walking towards the door I was stopped by a group of men with guns drawn. Cursing myself for not having my gun I looked to Journey for answers.

"Leaving so soon?" The voice sounded familiar, but I couldn't put a face to it. Turning to where I heard the voice, I came face to face with Paradise's father. "We meet again Kenneth." He went to shake my hand, but I didn't move. If I had my gun on me I could have easily taken all of them out. Pussy was on my mind and I wasn't thinking. I cursed myself for the dumb ass mistake.

"What the fuck do you want. Why am I here?"

"You took something from me and I wanted it back. As long as you are alive, that will never happen." I went to speak and one of his men hit me over the head with the gun. I blacked out immediately. When I woke up, I was tied up in a room and they all came walking in. Happy wasn't the word, when I saw Paradise walk through the door. I don't know how she got with her father, but I was glad she was. That was until he started talking. I wanted to kill her father for telling her about my affair with Journey, but I had no idea she was pregnant. I guess I should have known that was going to happen because I never used protection. I felt like shit and I couldn't explain how I fucked up so bad. I had never seen Paradise cry until she stood there basically saying I didn't think she was good enough to carry my seed. I wanted to cut Journey's fucking head off and serve it to Paradise, but I couldn't. As bad as I fucked up, nothing could have prepared me for Sin walking through the door and her father telling me they had an affair. The love I had for Paradise made me understand that I pushed her into the arms of another man. The devil in me said there was no way I was letting that shit fly. That was the ultimate betrayal. I didn't even know Journey was her sister, so her fuck up was worse than mine. In my eyes, this bitch did the unforgivable. When they all cleared out the room, I tried to figure a way out of this. Not knowing how pissed Paradise was at me, I wondered if I could trick her into letting me go. I could not let these mother fuckers win. EVERYBODY HAD TO DIE.

SUAVE...

Some shit wasn't right and this time I wasn't taking any chances. Everything told me something wasn't right with my brother. It has now been 5 days and no one has heard from him or seen his ass. He hasn't found Paradise and he would not leave without her. The fucked up part is my brother moved in silence, so figuring out his last move would be hard. I called a meeting with the fellas at the warehouse. I didn't need the girls worrying that it was now some more shit going down. Especially Tank. She didn't want my ass to walk out the door. If I got up and went to the bathroom, she was on my heels. I understand she is scared of losing me, but I can't move like this. It was time to end this shit. This has dragged on long enough and I was over the shit. I turned my attention to the men in the room. Everyone was now here, I didn't like repeating myself and I needed everyone to be clear on what the fuck I was about to say.

"I don't have any proof, but I know something has happened to my brother. He does not move like this. If he had his girl back, I wouldn't be worried. He would never leave without her. I came here for one reason and that was to bring Paradise home. In the time that I have been here, I have been shot, kidnapped, Smalls was shot, and now my brother is gone missing. This is unacceptable. I will not tolerate incompetence. You are looking at me and I'm sure you are saying to yourself who the fuck this nigga think he is. Let me remind you, I am the silent killer. I'm the nigga that will peel the skin off your mother's whole body in your face. I'm the nigga that will feed you to my dogs while you're still alive. I'm the nigga that is not allowing any more fuck ups. When I handed all of this over to Smalls he told me he had a team of niggas that would get shit done. I'm just not seeing it. From this day forward, if I don't see results someone is going to die. I don't care if it's you or your daughter. You're afraid of the devil, but you should be afraid of me. I raised him. Now, you niggas have exactly 24 hours to bring me some useful information or somebody mama is going to be purchasing a black dress. Are we clear?" I looked around the room and all you could see was fear. That was what I needed. A scared mother fucker would sell his mama out to the nigga they were scared of.

"Suave, I know you said useful information, but what about that chick he was fucking with?" Lil Goon spoke up.

"The one he went away with?" I looked to Smalls.

"That was the last time anybody heard from him." That's what I'm talking about, results.

"Ok so what's the bitch name?" Nobody spoke up so I'm assuming nobody knew. I pulled my gun out and pointed it at one of the niggas in the crew. "I said useful information. If don't nobody know her name, then that is not useful. I guess yall think I was joking. Say your prayers lil homie."

"I don't know her name nigga, but I know where she lives." Smalls spoke up saving his boy's life. I dropped my gun and put it back on my waist.

"See, results."

"Let's go cancel that bitch like Nino." Smalls joked as me and him laughed walking out of the warehouse. The lil homies didn't find shit funny, but I didn't give a fuck. I needed answers and I didn't have any time to waste.

TANK...

Suave got me fucked up if he thinks I'm going to stay behind whenever he leaves the house. He has no idea I have been following him every time he leaves. I know he was too smart to let me trail him, so I wait for about 20 minutes and then track his phone to see where he is. I know some people may say I'm crazy, but I will not allow him to go missing again. Those months with him gone was almost unbearable and I wasn't going through that shit again. I parked a block away and crept up to the warehouse to see what the fuck was going on. I see they are still keeping secrets. None of us knew that Gangsta was missing. Hell, I didn't even know that he had a bitch. Hearing them say they were heading to her house, I hid in the damn bushes because they were on their way out the door. Once I knew they were gone, I crept back to my car and waited for him to get to his next destination so I could track him. Pulling my gun out of my glove box, I screwed on my silencer. I would have his back even when he didn't want me to. I wish I didn't have to sneak, but I know my man and he would beat my ass if he knew I was out here. At least he would be alive. I didn't give a fuck about anything else.

SUAVE...

Pulling up to Journey's house, me and Smalls twisted our silencers on and got out of the car. Breaking her door off the hinges we walked in and could tell she had left in a hurry. Stuff was thrown everywhere.

"Okay, look around for something to tell us where she could have gone. Don't take your gloves off. We don't need any mistakes." Smalls nodded his head in acknowledgement. I didn't know what I was looking for, but I would know it when I see it. Women were more careless than men. I looked at the pictures of her on the wall and I realized I had seen her somewhere before. Trying my best to place where I saw her, I came up with nothing and continued searching for answers. Looking around, it was pissing me off that I hadn't found anything yet. I needed to find this bitch, after seeing that she left in a hurry I knew she was the key to my brother's disappearance. Looking through her mail I stopped dead in my tracks. The shit finally came to me. Ain't this about a bitch.

"Smalls, let's go." He walked in the living room where I was standing.

"You find something?"

"Naw, I seen this bitch before. When me and Tank went to the police station to track Paradise's car. She was out there talking. This bitch a police officer. I'm about to call my connect on the inside and see if she has any other addresses listed." We walked out and got back in my whip. Calling the officer I had on payroll, I had to convince him to give me the info.

"I will make it worth your while. 100k for the information." He got quiet for a second.

"Hold on, but you better not leave any evidence behind. My ass is on the line here."

"When have you ever known for me to leave anything behind."

"You're right, I'm just making sure. Give me a minute to pull her file." After about 10 minutes he gave me her mother's address. I told him I would see him with his payment later and we headed to the address he had given me.

"You think she went there?" Smalls asked.

"I don't know, but if she didn't I'm sure her mother can tell us where she is. If she doesn't well you know what happens after that. "We rode the rest of the way in silence. I'm sure we both were thinking the same thing at this moment. We couldn't lose anybody else to this madness. It was time to end this and I was done playing with these mother fuckers.

"We pulled up to her mother's house and ringing the doorbell was out of the question. If she is in there, they aren't trying to answer any doors. Smalls checked the window and it was open. Climbing in, he came and unlocked the door for me and I walked in. You can hear voices coming from the kitchen.

"I told you that he was evil and not to deal with him. You just don't listen. I am not getting involved in this mess. I'm sorry, you know that I love you, but you have to leave. He is not just going to let you walk away like that. You know too much." It sounded like the mother was going off.

"Well that's good to know. I need to know everything you know." They turned around and looked at us horrified.

"Who are you and what are you doing in my house?" The mother was pissed, but her day was about to get worse.

"Who am I? That depends on who you ask. Right now, I am the person who decides if you live or die today. I'm going to be honest, it's not looking good for you. Your daughter here was the last person to see my brother and I know she has something to do with his disappearance." I walked over to her knife set and grabbed the butcher knife. Smalls grabbed a bag of chips off the counter and opened them.

"Really nigga?" We both laughed. I swear all that nigga do is eat. "Now, you are going to tell me what you know or it's going to get real messy in here." The mother looked at her and started in.

"Journey tell them now." I can tell Journey didn't want to say anything, so I gave her some initiative. I raised my gun and shot her mother in the head.

"See, the problem is you are more afraid of whoever it is you are working for, but I promise, you are fearing the wrong person. I know in your mind you are thinking what's the worst that could happen? He already killed my mother and he can shoot me, but that's not what is about to happen. I am going to show you why you need to fear me and then you are going to tell me what I need to know." Tears were flowing from her eyes, but I didn't care. I grabbed the butcher knife and walked over to her mother. Grabbing her arm, I chopped it off. Journey screamed out in horror. I ignored her and I walked to the cabinets and grabbed a plate. Sitting the arm on the plate, I placed it in front of Journey.

"Eat." Looking at me like I had lost my mind, she shook her head no. "I will chop off every part of your mother's body and make you watch. Now eat." Crying uncontrollably, she lifted the arm and started biting it.

"Something is wrong with you niggas." Smalls yelled out as he looked on.

"Nigga you tried to make Na Na eat her own hand." Thinking about it he laughed.

"You right. My bad carry on." I turned back to Journey and waited for her to take a few more bites.

"I will make you eat your mother's entire body if you don't tell me what I need to know. Do you understand?" She nodded her head yes. "Where is my brother?"

"My father approached me and had me date him and told me when the time was right, he wanted me to bring him there. I didn't know that he intended to kill him." She was crying hysterically now, but I didn't' give a fuck. I continued my questioning. I didn't give a fuck about her tears.

"Who is your father?"

"Louis Garzon." I turned and looked at Smalls as he choked on his chips.

"You're Paradise's sister?"

"Yes, but I didn't know that I had a sister. She is there as well." Now I was confused. I thought Sin had Paradise.

"Okay, I need for you to tell me everything you know because this shit not making sense."

After hearing everything Journey had to say, I was speechless. Talk about a double cross. Grabbing my gun, I pointed it at Journey's head since I no longer needed her, but she stopped me.

"I'm pregnant with Gangsta's baby. Please don't kill me. He will never forgive you if you killed his seed." I know my brother and we would definitely go to war over that. I would do the same. Lowering my gun, I was about to talk it over with Smalls to see what he thinks I should do when Journey's head snapped back. Looking at the blood pour from the bullet hole that was now in her forehead, I looked at Smalls like what the fuck nigga. He shrugged his shoulders clueless.

"Didn't I tell you we're not accepting nobody else's kids. I don't think Paradise would be too happy to be raising someone else's, let alone her sister's baby by her man. What the fuck are you thinking?" Tank was standing in the kitchen now rubbing her belly.

"What are you doing here?" This girl was something else.

"Nigga if you thought for one second, I was letting you out of my sight you had me fucked up. What's in here to eat? This baby is hungry." Smalls handed her some of his chips, I couldn't do shit but shake my head at both of them.

"Alright, it's time to go. Smalls, call the crew we need a meeting with everybody. Tank, wipe down anything you touched and let's go."

"Hold on bae." Tank raised her gun and shot Journey 5 times in her stomach. "I told you I'm not taking no chances on some ugly ass baby coming back to life. Now let's go." We got the fuck out of there and headed to our meeting.

GANSTA...

These niggas think whooping my ass was going to bother me they had me fucked up. If they were smart, they would raise their guns and put a bullet in my head. One mistake and this shit was going to go really bad for their ass. I zoned out as the next nigga took his turn and started punching me. I could barely see out of my eyes and all I could think about was how I was going to take each of their ass out.

"What the fuck are you waiting on? Kill me. Don't play with it. I thought you was supposed to be the head of the Cartel, but you are a bitch." Louis walked up to me and pulled my finger back until it broke. That shit hurt like a mother fucker, but I wasn't going to give him the satisfaction of screaming out in pain.

"Trust me, you are going to die. I just want you to suffer before you do. With every hit, I want you to regret the day you laid eyes on Paradise. I want to break you. I want you to beg for forgiveness and once you have been reduced to nothing, then I will kill you." He walked out leaving his men to beat the shit out of me some more. He was waiting on me to break, but that will never happen. He wasn't as smart as he thought he was. You don't give the devil time to take over your house. Even God kicked Lucifer out.

8- RUN THIS TOWN

"Feel it coming in the air. Hear the Screams from everywhere, I'm addicted to the thrill. It's a dangerous love affair, can't be scared when it goes down. Got a problem tell me now, only thing that's on my mind is, who's gone run this town tonight?" Jay z

PARADISE...

I couldn't believe I had a fucking sister. I wonder if my mother knows? At this point it didn't even matter. Regardless of what my father said, I was going to kill her. There was no way I was going to allow this bitch to have a baby by my man. I never thought I would see the day I would have to go to war with my own father, but that's exactly what was about to happen. He ruined my fucking life and I could not allow him to get away with it. I had been mapping out a plan. When the time was right I would get the fuck out of here. I only hoped I would be able to save G. He did me dirty, but I did him worse. Too much may have been done for us to get back together, but I would do my best to get him out of here alive. He doesn't deserve this. The only thing I was afraid of was if he would take my ass out once I freed him. I trained him, but the devil was already inside of him. And one thing I learned along the way is, you don't cross a monster unless you plan to take him out. Shaking my head at the mess I created, I got up to get in the shower so I could set my plan into motion.

SUAVE...

Looking around the room, I saw a bunch of unsure faces. Fear engulfed everyone sitting in this room. They were looking to me for answers, but I didn't have any. I didn't know what would happen on tomorrow, but I did know we were done standing down. They all would have a choice. I was about to ask them to do something they probably never dreamed of doing.

"I brought you all here tonight because it is time for us to go to war." I let that sink in before I continued. "When I came back we had one goal and that was to bring Paradise home safe, but it is no longer safe for us. I have no answers for you as to why the Garzon Cartel is trying to take us out, but what I do know is this. They will not win. This is our streets. Our sets. Our women. Our brothers. Our families. They have crossed the line and showed us they will stop at nothing to take us down. Are you willing to allow everything you worked so hard for be taken by some old Columbian mother fucker? Or are you going to fight for what's yours? I will not force you to go to war, but if they come for you or any of your family we will not back you. If you are in and down to ride stay seated. If you choose to not fight with us, you may leave now." Everyone stayed seated except the lil homie Frog.

"No offence to anybody in this room, but I have never killed anybody before and I damn sure have never went to war with a Cartel. I sell drugs that's what I do. If it ain't about the money it doesn't make sense." I nodded at him and allowed him to leave.

"Tank, I know you want in, but you are going to sit this one out. We will discuss this more at home. Everybody else go enjoy your families. On tomorrow we will show these mother fuckers who run this town.

FROG...

These niggas had me fucked up if they thought I was going to war over Gangsta's ass. I don't even like the nigga. He is rude and disrespectful as fuck. They ain't going to protect us no way. All they give a fuck about is their own circle. I'm not trying to die fucking with these niggas over a bitch. I just wanted to get money. Unlocking my door, I walked in my crib and all the lights were off. Which is strange because so many people live here, somebody always up. Grabbing my gun I turned on the lights.

"Who the fuck are you and why are you in my house? Where the fuck is my family?" Some old nigga was sitting on my couch.

"I am Louis Garzon. I believe I am the one you and your crew is planning on taking out." Waiting for me to respond, he crossed his legs and just looked at me.

"I wasn't about to do shit. That's why I'm here and not there. Where is my family?"

"I had my guys take them out to dinner. They are fine. I just want to talk. I need to know the plans and when they are planning to come. I will pay you for the information."

"I don't know anything accept they are coming. I just told you I left."

"Well, I need for you to tell them that you are in. Once you find out what they are going to do then you call me and tell me."

"I ain't no snitch. Just because I didn't want to ride with them doesn't mean I will rat them out."

"I will pay you 1 million dollars after you give me the information I need. I'm sure they weren't going to pay you to go to war, but was going to ask you to risk your life. What I am offering will set you and your family up for life and you will be nowhere near the war." Thinking it over, I didn't need any more convincing.

"I'm in. What's the number you want me to call."

SMALLS...

I knew that Nik was about to be pissed. This war was not like the shit in the hood. We knew who and what we were up against in these streets. We moved accordingly and always came out on top. Our crew has been blessed, but we lost some good niggas along the way. I didn't want to be one of those niggas, but I had to ride with Suave. There was no way I wasn't going. We have been down for each other for years. I was 14 the day I met Suave. Some niggas were trying to rob me and they had every intention on killing me, until Suave came out of nowhere and aired they ass out. I was just a young nigga trying to make money. I didn't bother anybody and that's where mother fuckers got it twisted and thought shit was sweet. I wasn't like G and Suave, but I was just as deadly. I don't know what demons them niggas have inside of them, but I'm glad they ass was on my side. Suave and his crew took me under their wings and showed me the ropes. I was a hot head, but I was teachable. I have been loyal to my nigga since the day he saved my life and I will forever be. Turning his whole organization over to me without a thought, Suave has always had my back and I will always have his. There was no way I was allowing him to go to war without me. I walked in our bedroom and my girl was laying there looking like a big ass whale. It was almost time for my baby to arrive. After losing a child, I was scared to give that much of myself to someone again. But I was willing because I loved Nik. I knew her bald headed ass was about to go off, but I run this shit.

"Baby, are you woke? We need to talk." She turned over to me and there were tears in her eyes.

"Tank already told me. I can't believe you are about to do this and I'm due in a couple of weeks. You are about to be a father and we need you here."

"Listen, the life I live is dangerous. I could be taken out any day. You knew what the fuck it was when you started dating me. I been a father and losing Ariel was the hardest thing I ever had to do in life. If I don't go and put an end to this shit, I will be risking losing all of that again. I can't have that shit. I won't go through that again."

"Don't act like you are doing this for us. You are doing this for them. You are selfish and I'm tired of this." Getting pissed I started rubbing my temples.

"What the fuck do you mean? THEY ARE US. We are a fucking family. If they come for one, they come for us all. I live these streets and the reality is they will probably bury me. I'm not Suave, I will never walk away. As much as I love you I won't lie to you. So, either you can walk away or you can continue to ride for a nigga."

"You know damn well I ain't going nowhere, but your ass better come back to me or I promise I'm going to dig your ass up and beat the shit out of you."

"You know damn well I'm coming back. Who else gone spend all that money on your ass some wigs? Your bald head ass cost money." Hitting me on my arm she laughed at me. I loved her, but I was dead ass serious. I was praying the baby got my hair. My bitch hair was nappy as shit, the little bit she got. Laughing to myself, I leaned over and kissed her on her stomach. It was a lot on my mind, but that didn't mean I wasn't going to get any pussy. Sliding down I started sucking on her clit. I wasn't in the mood for no love making. I was about to tear her ass up. All I could do was pray to God she didn't go into labor. Lifting her legs back as far as I could, I slid my tongue up and down her slit and then went to her ass. I started sucking on that mother fucker like it was a chicken bone. Nik ass started moaning like crazy. I loved when she did that because it made my dick brick hard. I was a nasty nigga and I didn't give a fuck who knew it. Once her juices soaked my face, I knew she was ready for this dick. I stood up and slammed my dick in her. That's what I loved most about Nik, she didn't give a fuck what I did. She was going to take it and throw that shit back. That's exactly what she did. Grinding her pussy up under me, I went to work. Rubbing her clit as I stroked her, she came instantly on my shit. I wasn't done though.

"Turn over." She waddled her ass up and did as I instructed. Rubbing my dick against her ass, I slid it straight in. Each time she threw that ass back on me, I slapped that mother fucker. Feeling my dick swell I knew it was time for me to let that first one ride. As my body shook, I released all my seeds in her ass. Laying on my back, I caught my breath as I got ready for round two.

"Come get this dick back hard." She crawled over to me licking her lips.

TANK...

Leaving the warehouse with bae ass so much was on my mind. I knew this was something that had to be done, but there was no way I was going to sit back and allow them to go without me. I let him think shit was cool, but on the inside I was pissed. If it wasn't for me, his ass wouldn't even be here to go to war. These niggas will never learn that we are just as hood as them. I know I'm pregnant, but I would rather be out there by my nigga side with guns blazing than at home not knowing if he was coming back to me. I looked over to him and I could tell he had shit he was thinking about as well. They had his brother, I knew there was no way I could convince him not to go. He just wasn't going alone, little did he know. This was going to affect our family as a whole, and I think everybody should have a chance to be there. Finally, he broke the silence.

"I know what you are thinking, but you are not going. You are pregnant and I told you before, you are not a street nigga. Whatever you did before me, is now of the past."

"Suave, I am your other half. Not your fucking child. How many times have I told you that you can't tell me what to do? Quit trying to control me and let me ride with you." He didn't respond, but I knew he was pissed. His jaw line was moving fast as shit. He pulled up to a park and stopped the car.

"Get out and take a walk with me." I could feel a lecture coming and I really didn't want to hear it, but I got out and decided to stand for what I believed. "For some reason, you think you have a choice." Pausing, he looked at me I guess to try and put fear in me. "I gave you an order and I am not in the mood for your shit. For once, you are going to do as you are told."

"I don't know who the fuck died and made you my daddy. Last I checked I didn't know who he was and I didn't need anybody taking his place. You can't expect me to sit here and go thru what I just did. How dare you?"

"Lashay, calm your fucking voice down. I don't have to be your ugly ass daddy, I am your husband and I told you to stand down." Walking up to his face, I leaned in to make sure he saw every word that was about to come out of my mouth.

"And I told you, I don't give a fuck what you are saying. You don't run me. I'm not scared of you or anything that you are about. Remember that." Before I could say anything else, the nigga had grabbed me by my neck so fast, I couldn't react. He was choking the snot out of me and it was nothing I could do about it. Clawing at his hands, I tried my best to get him to let me go. Unsuccessful, all I ended up with was some nails full of skin. I couldn't breathe and I felt light headed as shit. I looked at him, begging him to stop with my eyes, but when I looked into his, my soul shivered. There was nothing there. I had unlocked something inside of him that I never seen before. Feeling myself black out, I couldn't believe I was about to die by the hands of the man I loved with all of me. He snatched me to him and I'm thinking, what else is left to say? I was dizzy as fuck when I felt his lips touch mine. Barely able to open my eyes, I looked at him and Suave was back. He let go the grip he had on my neck, but he still held it as he kissed me. I was so scared, I didn't know whether to kiss him back or run for dear life. Feeling my hesitation, he started telling me what to do again.

"Kiss me Lashay." I wanted to tell him to go jerk his dick off with a sock, but I opened my mouth allowing him to slide his tongue in. As he kissed me, he slid his free hand in my leggings and started caressing my clit and the juices came falling down like London bridges. The mixture of fear and pleasure was turning me the fuck on. Letting my neck go, he slid my leggings down, removing one of the legs to have access. He sat down on the swing and pulled his dick out.

"Come ride this mother fucker." Climbing on top of him, I stuck my legs through the ropes for leverage. Kissing me again, he slid his dick inside of me. I was trying to get a pace going, but I was slipping on the sand.

"Ride this dick or we are going to have a problem." Scared of what might happen if I didn't get it together, I dug my feet in the sand and started riding that dick like my life depended on it. All you could hear in the night air were my moans and the sound of my pussy talking. Then he started pushing off. The nigga actually began swinging with me riding his dick. Knowing I didn't have any more leverage as we swung back and forth, he gripped me by my ass cheeks and started pushing me back and forth. The motion of us going back and forth, mixed with him guiding my ass made the friction so intense I came immediately. My moans have now turned to screams because he has not let up. Placing his hands under my ass, he started lifting me up and down in the air as we swung back and forth. The shit was driving me crazy. After about 5 more minutes, I came again. Knowing my man like I do, I could tell he was about to cum. His swinging slowed down and then he stopped us all together. Standing me up, he sat back down on the swing.

"Suck my dick until every drop of cum in me is gone and you better not waste none." Sliding down to my knees I took him whole. One thing I knew how to do was suck a dick. Licking my tongue across his balls every time I deep throated him was sending him over the edge. The last time I went back down I slid his balls in my mouth at the same time. While his dick filled my entire throat, I swallowed causing my throat muscles to tighten on his dick.

"Fuck girl. Suck this dick." Working up a rhythm, I started sucking his shit like a porn star. Using both hands to massage him, as I sucked on his tip I could feel the pre cum on my tongue and his dick swelling.

"Baby I'm about to cum." I wanted to say I know, because I'm the shit, but I couldn't, his dick was down my throat. Instead, I just prepared for his seeds to slide down. When I felt him cum in my mouth, I kept going until he was shuddering and there wasn't a drop of cum or air left to come out that mother fucker. Standing up, I slid my leggings back on and waited for him to get his self together.

"Suave come on, you can sleep at home. I got sand and shit stuck on my knees. I need to take a shower." He opened his eyes and laughed as he got his self together.

"Tank don't make me kill your ass. Don't cross me or you are going to regret it." I continued to walk in silence. I didn't want to promise him because I knew I would break it. I would be there whether he wanted me to or not.

9- IS THIS THE END

"Momma told me one day it was gonna happen, but she never told me when. She told me it would happen when I was much older wish it would have happened then. Is this the end? Just can't let go. I just don't know. Is this the end?" Twista

TANK...

If Suave knew about my secret meeting he would beat my ass for sure. Some would call me hard headed, but I didn't give a fuck. I was not his child and I was grown and could make my own decisions. This was something I had to do for me. I chose to fight side by side with my man whether he wanted me to or not. As long as my family was in jeopardy, I was in hood mode. Looking around at my bitches, I knew that I was asking them to risk their lives and I wasn't sure how this would play out. It was only Shay and Bay Bay here, Nik was too far along in her pregnancy and I couldn't get her to slap a bitch let along go to war. After allowing them to get settled, I began my speech I had been rehearsing in my head all day.

"On last night, we found out that Gangsta is being held by the Garzon Cartel. His girl's father has him and his intentions are to kill him. Me and G have had our fair share of run ins and I know it seems weird that I'm ready to go to war for him, but it's not him that I'm choosing to fight for.

My husband will be out there on the front line and as long as he is at war, I'm at war." I looked at them before I continued, not sure how they would take the next thing I was about to say. "I was instructed to stand down, but you know I can't do that. I know you both have your own thing going on, but if I'm at war I need my bitches by my side.

They keep saying we should stay in our place, but I thought a woman's place was beside her man? All I know is I'm not a stand down kind of bitch and I know you aren't as well. We get mother fucking results. I hope my hoes are ready to rock if I'm rolling, but if you aren't, I definitely understand why."

"Girl, I was ready when you said war with the cartel. My life been so damn dry since you been gone. My damn guns done collected dust. The most action I got was when we saved G ass the last time and he beat your ass for helping him." Thinking back to that day I couldn't do shit, but laugh at Shay's joke. I couldn't believe they were mad we saved their lives. Looking over at Bay Bay, I waited to see what she was going to say.

"Bitch you already know I'm down. I ain't never backed down from a fight and I'm not about to start today. What's the plan?"

"That's the tricky part. I don't know where they are going. I have a tracker on Suave's phone, but I have to wait until he is there to track it. Basically, we are going to be arriving to the party late than a mother fucker."

"That could be bad for us. We won't know what we are walking into." Shay made a great point.

"Or, it could be great for us. If Suave and them are already there and going to war, they won't be expecting us. It's like we are their secret weapon, but they don't know it." I got exactly what Bay Bay was saying. If the Cartel didn't know that we were coming, they wouldn't expect us to come in blazing. That leaves them at a disadvantage.

"Okay cool. Go home and grab your shit. We will meet back here in 2 hours. I have to wait until Suave leaves or he will know something is up.

"Aight. That means I got time to get some dick." We looked at Shay and bust out laughing. "Hey, this could be my last time. I need to go happy if I'm going to go." We continued to laugh at her ass until we got in our separate cars and pulled off. I know she was laughing, but I'm sure it was some truth to it as well. This could be the last time either of us saw any of our family or friends. I just prayed we all came out on top. I drove back to the house to play mad. It was time to put my game face on and act like I had no intentions of going against his word.

SMALLS...

Today was the fucking day and I was more excited than scared. Whenever it was time to go to war, I turned into a different nigga. If you out here with fear in your heart, it could cloud your judgment and your actions. Scared mother fuckers will be out here shooting lil ass guns while hiding behind bricks. I was trying to knock niggas heads back. We had to make sure there was nobody left. If anyone was left alive, they could come back and avenge their crew. I wasn't having that shit. This was going to end today or I was going to die trying. I had a get ready for war routine that I always did. First I would eat only light foods. Then I would work out like crazy. Lastly, I would bust a nut. Not having sex with my girl though, I needed to clear my head not get lazy and go to sleep. In the midst of me getting my head right, my phone rings.

"What up Frog? You good?"

"I thought it over and I want to go with yall. I wouldn't be able to sleep at night if something happened to my niggas and I was at home safe and chilling. You feel me?"

"Yeah, I feel you. We are actually heading out in a minute. I'll come grab you and then we can meet the rest of the crew at the warehouse to go over the plan one more time."

"That's what I'm talking about. We gotta be on point. Can't have shit happening. I ain't gone lie, I'm nervous, but shit gone work out."

"Absolutely. Now get the fuck off my line nigga and go get ready. I'll be there in 30." Hanging up, I shot Suave a text and continued my work out. I grabbed some warming KY jelly out of the drawer and laid down on my bed. Pulling my dick out I admired my shit while I rubbed the oil on. I had about 7.5 inches on my shit, but it was thick as fuck. That's what drove the hoes crazy. They love that feeling of you stretching them to capacity. Sliding my hand up and down my dick I damn near forgot the reason I was in hear beating off. That jelly had my shit feeling good. Just because I'm a cocky nigga and I love the way my shit was glistening, I rubbed my shit nice and slow. Looking at my shit get bigger and thicker made me feel like that nigga. Finally over my conceited moment, I went to work at the tip of my dick. The speed and the jelly had my shit sounding like it was going in and out some wet ass pussy. I could feel my nut rising, but the shit wouldn't come out. Not having time to play around with it, I started screaming for Nik to come in the room. She came bursting through the door like something was wrong.

"Nigga, I thought something happened and your nasty ass just in here beating your dick." She turned to walk back out the room when I stopped her.

"I need you to catch this nut for me. You know I need a clear head, but I can't fuck you or I'll be sleepy as fuck. The shit right there at the top I just need you to get it."

Looking at me go up and down on my dick must have made her wet. She walked over to me and moved my hand. Replacing it with hers, she began jerking me off. I closed my eyes and next thing I know she done deep throated me.

"Fuck girl. I told you I can't have this kind of session." Not responding she just kept deep throating me sucking it until it felt like I was in some pussy. In 2 minutes, I felt my nut rising again and shot it straight down her throat.

"I knew if I sucked it instead of jerking, you wouldn't take that long. Go do what you need to do and come back. I don't want to hear no bullshit." I almost said fuck that war. I was ready to dive into some pussy, but I got up and loaded up my bag with all the ammo I had in the house. Stepping out of the house for what may be my last time, I went to go grab Frog.

Pulling up to his crib, I waited for him to get in.

"You sure you want to do this my nigga?"

"Yeah I'm sure. Are you sure?" He never looked my way when he responded.

"I'm just giving you a chance to go your ass back in the house and leave well enough alone. This life ain't for everybody and I get that. Mother fuckers can't take the pressure."

"I ain't everybody and I damn sure can take whatever pressure comes my way. Drive nigga." I pulled off without any regrets. I gave him the chance he needed to walk away. He chose to move forward. Pulling up to the warehouse, I grabbed my bag out the trunk and headed in.

"Where the fuck is everybody. Niggas is always late." Frog said aggravated as hell.

"The only people that need to be in this room is already here." Frog turned to face Suave. I guess he didn't notice him sitting there. "The one thing I hate is a rat. Anybody who knows me, know that. Granted, you don't really know a nigga like that. So, I could have given you a pass. But, with everything that's going on, ain't no more passes." It always weirded me out that Suave was always calm. No matter the situation, the nigga never raised his voice.

"I ain't no fucking snitch. I don't know what yall niggas on, but I'm up out of here." Frog attempted to walk out.

"It's funny that you actually think you still have a choice. I just gave you the chance to go back in the house and leave this shit alone. You weak my nigga and I can't let you live." I was now pointing my gun at him. We weren't going to shoot him, but I needed him to turn his bitch ass back around.

"Ain't shit weak about me nigga. This crew is weak. This is how you pay a nigga who has been loyal to you? Fuck you."

"Nigga you are weaker than a bitch edges in micro braids. One thing I have never been, and that's a fool. When you walked out of the meeting I respected you for your decision. You meant every word you said and I honored it. The moment you called me, I could hear it all in your voice that you were on some set up shit. We been in these fucking streets too long to not know a rat when we see one." Not giving a fuck about this nigga screaming loyalty, I grabbed him and placed him in a chair. Tying him up, all I could do was pray for his soul. I had no idea what Suave was about to do, but I knew it wasn't about to be pretty.

Waiting on the end result, Suave walked over to the door and let his dogs out. This was something I knew I didn't want to see. I don't know where the fuck he got them dogs from, but they were straight savages. I hated them mother fuckers. Covering his mouth with tape, Suave grabbed his knife and started carving into the nigga. You would think I would be used to this shit by now, but I wasn't. After severing pieces of his body, Suave walked towards the exit. Before walking out the door, the nigga turned around and only said one word.

"Eat." Them big head mother fuckers started tearing into his ass. Locking the door once we got out, I looked at that nigga and he didn't have a care in the world.

"Nigga you getting worse than Lucifer. I'm gone stop hanging with you mother fuckers." He laughed at my ass and got in his car. Pulling up beside me he yelled out the window.

"See you on the other side brother." I nodded my head and drove towards the last war I might ever fight.

SUAVE...

Driving to the mansion, it was so much on my mind. Tank thinks I just want to be back out here jeopardizing our family and she is wrong. This is the last thing I want to be doing, but my brother needs me. I never got the chance to tell him I was proud of him, I never got the chance to really thank him for all his help. I was the only father he ever acknowledged, even though our father was in the house. I raised him and what kind of man would I be if I left him out here? The fucked up nigga in me wants to take everybody out that crossed him, but I know I can't do that. I'm sure he is pissed now, but he would never forgive me if I killed Paradise. If he chooses to take her out, he can do that his self. I wasn't touching that. No matter what I would make sure she gets out the house and they can handle their own shit. Given the opportunity, I was going to holla at my baby brother. I went through the exact same thing with Tank.

Having to forgive someone you love and they crossed you to this compacity is hard, but it is possible. It fucked me up more when I almost lost Tank. The minute she started fighting for her life, I forgave her. My brother was gone have to do the same. I know he loves her. Hell, he done damn near murdered everybody to get to her. He was more stubborn than I was, but I hope he can get passed it. Thinking about this and about to reach my destination, I decided to call my wife.

"Hey baby, what are you doing?" I asked knowing damn well she was at home pissed.

"Nothing, in here talking to Nik. We about to call my granny over here to have prayer service and pray for you niggas."

"I never turn down a prayer, but I will be okay. I told you, I will always come back to you. No matter what. You just have to believe that. I haven't made it 40 years being a dummy."

"Nobody said you was dumb, just bring your ass home. And baby, just remember that you love me. Okay."

"Okay. See you soon." When I hung up, her words seemed to be echoing in the car. Just remember that you love me. Not having time to try and decipher the shit, I got out and grabbed my shit out the trunk. Waiting on the others to pull up I took my shirt off and put on my bullet proof vest. Placing my shirt back on, the other cars began to pull up.

"Nigga don't nobody want to see that flimsy ass chest. Fuck is you doing?" Smalls always had a joke or two. We about to go to war and this nigga playing and shit.

"Nigga what do it look like? Bring your ass on before them mother fuckers see us."

"I'm coming, but your box body built ass better have me one. If I get shot, I'm telling Nik your ass had a vest and didn't give a fuck about anybody else." Reaching in my trunk, I pulled out a box and sat it on top of the car.

"Nigga I always take care of my people. Everybody got one. Now let's go." Everybody got out of their cars and started getting war ready. After passing out extra guns and vests, we were now ready. I looked to my men and decided to give a quick pep talk. Some of them looked worried.

"I know this may be the biggest war some of you will ever fight, but we got you." I emphasized pointing at me and Smalls. "I know that I am here for my brother and his girl, but I do know that without any of you this is not possible. I will do everything in my power to make sure everyone gets back home to their families. Stay smart, pay attention, and show no mercy. If it's not Gangsta or Paradise, drop them and keep it moving. Try to go for all head shots. Watch out for each other and let's get this over with." We all drew our guns and headed to the mansion on foot.

TANK...

After hanging up the phone with Suave, I jumped out of my bed and started getting dressed. Since we were going to war I made sure I dressed the part. First, I grabbed a comb and braided my shit straight to the back. Then I grabbed my black hoodie and black jogging pants and threw them on. I opened my closet and grabbed a pair of black J's. As I was closing the closet, it dawned on me that I was going to war. Putting my J's back, I grabbed my black Tims and suited up. While I was tying my boots up, Nik came in the room talking shit.

"Tank, please don't do this. We almost lost you once and we just got Suave back. You will only be a distraction."

"I know you mean well, but I am not about to keep explaining myself. This is not up for discussion. As I explained to my husband on last night, I would rather be beside him guns drawn. Being here not knowing what's going to happen is far worse. If he is in trouble I can save him. If shit is going bad we can think together. I don't expect anybody to understand that and quite frankly I don't give a fuck if yall do. You want to help me, pray we all come back alive and in one piece." Standing up, I looked at her to see if she was done.

"You don't have to catch an attitude. That's your problem, nobody can't tell you shit. I hope for your sake, everybody does make it out."

"Are you finished? I need to head out and meet the bitches." Not giving her a chance to respond I walked out of the room and out of the house. I headed over to the warehouse where me and the girls were supposed to meet up.

When I got there, they were already sitting outside the truck waiting on me.

"What the fuck took you so long? My nerves shot to shit and you playing in your ass. You will let a bitch think some shit over and change her mind." Laughing at Shay, I threw a joke back at her ass.

"I know your ass ain't talking. It takes you 3 hours to get ready and we only be going to Chilis. Let's go before we miss all the action. We jumped in the whip and headed to the location I had tracked on Suave's phone.

GANGSTA...

It was that time again when Louis and his men were in here fucking me up. This time he was trying to break me for something else. He wanted a location on Smalls. That would never happen. I didn't care if he chopped up every part of my body, I would never give up my nigga. I'm sure he knows that, he just wants to release some frustrations because he can't find him.

"I'm going to ask you again, where does your gutter rat of a friend lay his head?"

"And I told you, he lives in deez nuts." Grabbing a hammer, he hit me in the hand with it. I don't know if the adrenaline had me pumped up or if I was truly Lucifer, because the shit didn't even hurt. I was just ready for this to be over with. Shit was getting old. Pissed off that I didn't even flinch, he put on some brass knuckles and went to work on my face. I could only imagine how I looked right now. The image in my mind made me laugh. All I could see is the episode of Martin when he was on the ropes telling Gina "I don't wanna fight no mo." I hadn't realized I laughed out loud until he started screaming in my face.

"You think this shit is funny? I will show you funny. You have exactly one hour to tell me where Smalls lives, or I will kill Paradise right in front of you." I don't know if he was bluffing, but my whole insides shifted when he said that. Even though I didn't give him a reaction, that shit just fucked me up.

"Do what you feel you have to do. You have to live with that, not me. The bitch was sleeping with my best friend. You better call him up, maybe he will give a fuck about the shit you spitting, because I don't." I was bluffing like a mother fucker and I prayed he didn't call it. Walking out the room, I could tell he was pissed. Now alone, I started thinking how the fuck could I get out of this shit.

PARADISE...

Freshly showered, I knew it was time for my father's security to bring me my dinner. I laid under the covers naked as the day I was born. Working for my father and partnering with G, I have learned that even the toughest nigga got took out over some pussy. Something about that shit that made niggas stupid. Hearing the door unlock, I removed my covers and pretended to be asleep. I could tell somebody was standing over me and just watching. Making it seem like I was just waking up, I acted startled when I saw the guard standing there.

"What the fuck are you doing? Are you crazy?"

"I'm sorry. I didn't know what to say to you. Here is your food. I will leave you to it. I apologize again." Stumbling over his words, he walked over to hand me my plate. I looked him dead in the eyes and started playing with my pussy. Dropping his eyes to my wet girl, you could damn near see the slob dripping from his lips.

"Close the door. We have to be quick, I don't want anybody to catch us. Do you know how to give a quickie?" Rubbing his dick through his pants, I waited on him to give me an answer. He never gave one, he walked to the door and closed it. Walking back over to me, he laid the plate on the dresser and got on his knees. Home boy didn't waste any time diving in. The shit wasn't all that, but I wasn't trying to bust a nut anyway. I had one goal in mind and that was to figure out a way to get his gun. Trying to remember to fake moan, I kept thinking of a plan in my head.

"Mmmm yeah. That's it daddy. I knew you were a beast." If he took his clothes off I could get ahold of it then. Needing him to be naked, I faked an orgasm. "Ooh shit. I'm about to cum. Oh yes, that's it right there." After a couple of fake jerks, he stood up and looked to me like what's next. "I know you didn't do all of that and didn't plan on giving me none of that dick."

"I don't have a condom." He tried to explain without talking his way out of some pussy.

"I'm on birth control. It's fine. Hurry, I don't want us to get caught." Having no intentions on letting this nigga nut, I lied too quick. Sensing that he was about to change his mind, I leaned over and unzipped his pants. Pulling his dick out, I took him all the way in. Now that it was hard, the nigga was only about 5 inches and that's if you stretched that mother fucker.

"Damn baby. You deep throated this big ass dick." Damn near choking from laughter, I played it off as if I was gagging from it being so big. Moaning as I sucked him, I reached up and started playing with his balls at the same time. He got so into it, that he leaned back and closed his eyes. Easing my hand closer and closer to his waist, I would grab it as soon as he began to nut. As big as he was, I knew he was a softy. He would go crazy once he came. Making the shit extra sloppy, I could feel his dick swelling in my mouth. Releasing his seeds in my mouth, I spit them back on his dick and kept sucking. I was not about to swallow this nigga's nut. Making sure to keep going until he was too weak to stand, I slid the gun from its holster as he fell onto the bed. *POP. POP.POP.* All you could hear were gunshots going off all around the mansion causing him to jump up off the bed and reach for the gun. I immediately fired at his ass. Whatever was going on almost fucked up my plan. 30 seconds earlier and I would have been sucking lil dick for nothing. Hurrying up, I threw on my clothes and eased out the door to try and get the fuck out of here alive.

SUAVE...

The element of surprise worked in our favor. We used our guns with the silencers on them to take out the niggas that was guarding the outside of the mansion. That allowed us the shock factor when we came busting through the mother fucker blazing. After taking out the guards downstairs, I instructed for half of the crew to go upstairs and search the rooms. Me, Smalls, and Goon was taking down. Going through each room we blasted anything that moved. Entering into what appears to be Louis's Office I knew this was where they had G. Journey had already told us everything. What she didn't tell us, was how the fuck to get into the secret room

"Goon, you look out and make sure no one is coming. If anybody approach this door blow their wig back. No questions. Smalls you help me find out how the fuck to get in the secret room." Everyone did as they were told. I had no idea how to get the fuck on the other side of the wall.

"We may have to find Louis bitch ass and make him open the shit." I whispered to Smalls.

"Yeah, let's get the fuck out of here and see if there is another way in. I'm going to take this picture though." Smalls walked over to some art that was hanging on the wall.

"Nigga how the fuck are you going to be in a shoot out grabbing shit? Make that make sense."

"Nigga, Nik is pissed my ass is here with you and I gotta make it up to her." He went to grab the picture and I stopped him.

"Mother fucker leave the damn picture."

"Aight, but if my girl can't have it he can't either." Grabbing the picture he threw it to the floor and the wall moved.

"I guess you wanting this ugly ass picture worked out in our favor." Slowly walking through the door guns first, we rounded the corner and G was sitting there fucked up.

"Damn nigga, you ugly as fuck right now." Smalls joked as always. Gangsta lifted his head up and opened his eyes.

"Either they done sent my ass to heaven, or they done beat me so bad I'm hallucinating." Looking at me, he didn't know what to believe.

"Nigga it's me in the flesh. Long story, but bring your ugly ass on. We gotta get the fuck out of this mansion." Untying him, I could feel him staring at me. "Dude, it's really me, now stop starting at me. You freaking me out looking at me with one eye and shit." Finally getting a laugh out of him, we headed for the door.

Once we made it back out to the main corridor, the rest of the homies were downstairs as well.

"No sign of Paradise, but there was a guard dead in a bedroom with his dick out." I already knew that was the work of Paradise. Heading out the door, we made it to the front lawn and the bullets started flying. They were coming at us from every angle. Passing G a gun, we all fired back. But it was too many of them. They were closing in on us and we had nowhere to go. Saying a silent prayer, I knew I had to take some of them mother fuckers with us. Right when we realized it was over for us and we were defeated, out of nowhere more shots rang out. I looked over to the side and there was Tank, gun blazing. She had her crew with her as usual and they were knocking the men down left and right.

"These bitches are crazy." Smalls shook his head in disbelief.

"Big brother I don't know what you are going to do with her ass, Tank thinks she is Al Capone." As mad as I was, I ain't gone lie this is the second time I was happy as fuck she went against my word. I would never let her know that, but I could fuck the shit out of her right now. Turning my attention back to the shooters, we helped the golden girls knock the rest of them down. Standing there looking stupid, she knew I was about to light into her ass.

"What the fuck did I tell your ass?"

"I know, but I felt it in my gut you would need me. I'm sorry, but I couldn't stand by and not know if you were going to come back to me."

"We will discuss this later, did you seen anybody leave out of the house?"

"No, we were out here when the shooting first started and we didn't see anyone." I looked over to Gangsta and he was heading back towards the house.

"Where the fuck are you going? I have no idea what was going through his mind.

"She didn't see anybody come out, that means Paradise is still in there." He damn near barked it at me. I knew there was no way I could stop him, so I let him go.

"Suave, if Paradise is still in there, that means her father is too. You know this nigga only working with one eye, so I'm going to go back in with him. You stay out here with the girls." Smalls instructed.

"Okay, yall be safe and hurry the fuck up." I watched them go back in and we all raised our guns just in case all these mother fuckers weren't dead. Out of nowhere we saw Paradise running across the lawn. I ran out to get her and make sure she made it to safety.

"Did you see G? He went back in for you, him and Smalls."

"No, I was hiding until I made sure the coast was clear. Did you all kill my papa?" She didn't show it in her face expression, but her eyes looked as if she was ready to cry.

"No, we didn't see him or you and we cleared the whole house."

"YOU HAVE TO GET HIM OUT OF THERE NOW. SUAVE GET G OUT OF THERE." I don't know what triggered her to go off.

"I have no way to get in touch with him. We have to physically go in."

"Suave if you didn't find my father that means he went through the tunnels. He has all of his houses triggered just in case someone comes in trying to take him out. The house is going to-..." Before she could finish her sentence the house exploded. I took off running towards the flames.

"Oh my God, no, no, no. This could not be happening." Someone pulled me to the ground.

"Baby, we have to go. I'm sorry, but we can't be here. We have to leave now." I looked up at Tank with tears running down my face. Getting up off the ground, I pulled myself together. I looked over at Paradise and she was crying hysterically, but I didn't give a fuck.

"I am going to find your father and I am going to kill him."

"Not if I find him first. Let's go." Just like that this bitch was no longer crying. The only other person I have ever seen turn their emotions off like that was G. Shit kind of gave me chills, but I couldn't worry about that now. We had to get the fuck away from here. I had Tank drive Small's car and we were out.

10- BEEF

"What's beef? Beef is when you make your enemies start your jeep. Beef is when you roll no less than 30 deep. Beef is when I see you. Guaranteed to be in ICU."
Notorious BIG

TANK...

Heading back to the house it was so much on my mind. I didn't know what the fuck just happened. One minute we were all safe and the next minute, Smalls and G got blew up in the house. My girl was about to have their child and her man was gone. I didn't even know how I would even break this to her. This was a pain I didn't wish on anybody. I also didn't want to go home to face the music with Suave. I know he was grateful, but he was going to fuck me up. I didn't care. That was an ass whooping I was ready to take. I did what I set out to do and that was have his back. We almost made it out of there as a whole family.

Pulling up to the house, I couldn't even stop the tears from flowing. The closer I got to the door, the more my heart ached. Walking in, I didn't have to say a word. She looked me in my eyes and she knew.

"Please Tank. Don't tell me that. Please, tell me he is in the hospital and he has a chance to make it." My silence only made her cry more. "What happened friend? Please God, not now. This can not happen now." I walked over and put my arms around her. I knew the exact pain she was feeling. I was just here. "Tank, you have to tell me what happened." Crying with her I explained it the best way I could.

"Everybody was cool and safe. We were about to leave and G went back to find Paradise. Smalls went with him and when we saw Paradise come out, we thought they were together. She started screaming go get him and the house blew up. I am so sorry. We had everybody and they went back in." She dropped to the ground. Just as I was thinking where the hell is everybody at, they walked through the door. I needed help with Nik. Suave walked over to her and hugged her. He was so stuck on comforting Nik, he didn't even close the door. We all stood there with the door open crying. They both lost someone and we all let them have their moment. Nik looked up and saw Paradise and she went crazy.

"It's all your fucking fault. GET THE FUCK OUT OF MY HOUSE. I DON'T WANT HER HERE. GET HER OUT OF HERE." Suave buried her face in his chest and allowed her to get it all out.

"It's not her fault friend. We have to come together. Let's grieve and mourn our family together." Grabbing Paradise's hand, I led her to the couch and we sat down. Suave started talking.

"My brother always wanted to be like me growing up. He never understood that I wanted him to be better than me. Nigga couldn't play dice to save his life. I took all that nigga money." Laughing, he wiped the tears from his eyes. "I have never seen a nigga eat as much as Smalls. Somebody could be getting their head sawed off and I swear he will stand there and eat. Nigga thought he was the funniest mother fucker around. He didn't take shit serious." I decided to join in talking about the memories we had of them.

"The first time I met Lucifer, I was scared as shit. Actually, I'm still scared of that nigga. He didn't even have to speak and I would know he was in the room. The hairs on my body would stand up. Now Smalls, I loved him from the start. He was crazy as fuck, but he kept us laughing."

"The first time I met G, I said this nigga is not crazy enough for me. I wanted a nigga on my level, but I ran into him later that day and the nigga ran a nigga over and killed him just to get me to call him." Paradise reminisced.

"I remember that day. I was mad as fuck. Matter fact, I was taking his money that day playing dice. I think he did that so he didn't have to pay me my money." Suave laughed as he thought back to that day.

"Nigga, I was gone pay you that petty ass money. I swear you got too much money to be that cheap." Our heads swung towards the door and there stood Gangsta and

Smalls. Screaming and crying tears of joy, we damn near knocked them over. All of us was trying to hug them at the same time.

"How the fuck did yall make it out? The mansion blew up." Everyone was thinking it, but Suave asked it.

"Because nigga, you can't kill Lucifer using fire." Nik was still standing there looking shocked. Smalls walked over to her and kissed her. The shit was too sweet. Everybody had a look on their face that looked like we were saying awwww. It wasn't the same reaction for Paradise and Gangsta though. He looked at her, but he didn't speak a word.

"I know this may be too soon to bring this up, but we only came to let you know that we were okay. We are leaving for Columbia on tomorrow. Paradise you are going with us. We don't know your city and I'm not trying to play find the Mexican. Nik I know you are hurting, but I'm okay. This war is not over until her father is dead. He will not stop until all of us are dead. I plan to make a burrito out of his ass first."

"Nigga first off, we are not Mexican with your silly ass and second, you won't get any resistance from me. My papa went too far this time and he has to be stopped. All I ask is let me be the one to do it. I need to do this for me and I don't want either of you to take that from me. He has ruined my life and now I will be the one to ruin his."

Paradise looked directly at G when she spoke, but he wouldn't even look up at her. Nik ran to the room crying. I knew the pain she was going through, but I understood what they needed to do. In order for this to be completely over, they had to end it. I just hoped we could survive one last time.

GANGSTA...

Running back into the mansion, the only thing on my mind was save Paradise. Even though I hated her ass right now, I refused to leave her with this psycho she called a father. As soon as me and Smalls ran in, we saw the old mother fucker running across the lawn. We went running out the side door trying to catch him. We barely made it to the middle of the yard when the explosion went off. I rolled over and watched him drive off with my good eye. I know the nigga wasn't going to stay away. He was leaving, but he would definitely be back. Looking back over to Smalls to make sure he was okay the nigga looked at me and laughed.

"You think I'm playing, but I swear you ugly as fuck right now. They fucked your ass up. I ain't never seen a nigga eye drooping like it was a tear drop."

"Your ass just don't know when to shut the fuck up. At least I'm ugly because I got beat, your ass just look like that." Laughing we got up and walked back around to the front. By the time we got there everybody was gone.

"I know them pussy mother fuckers didn't leave us. They didn't even check the ashes to see if we were still alive and I kept Suave's dusty ass ashes for a week." Smalls continued to talk shit.

"My car is parked over there. You forgot I drove here thinking I was about to get some pussy. Speaking of Journey I gotta find that bitch." I pulled my keys out of my pocket and we climbed in the car.

"That's what your ass get. You damn near drug me up the stairs for that bitch, but she dead than a mother fucker anyway."

"How did yall find her?"

"Suave knew the bitch. He said she was a cop. We went to her mom's house and she was there. Suave killed the mother, hey yall niggas are sick as fuck. He made that bitch eat her own mama." Looking at him tell the story, I burst out laughing. He always talking about how crazy we are, but he always got his ass right there. "He was about to let her live because she was pregnant, but Tank came through the door and killed the bitch."

"I swear my brother gone have to put a leash on that girl, she is out of control. Even though I don't like the shit she be doing, I'm glad her ass didn't listen to us with any of this shit and she saved me the trouble of killing that bitch and her baby."

"She told on your ass too. Suave said he fucking you up. I told you he was going to beat your ass."

"NIGGA SHUT UP DAMN." This was my nigga I swear. He kept me laughing. Getting out of the car, we thought some shit went down. The front door was wide open. Easing up to the door to assess the situation, we didn't say shit or make a sound. Listening to them talk, I whispered to Smalls.

"What the fuck is they doing?"

"Looks like we at our own funeral my nigga. They think we dead. Now we are the ghost." Nigga was still on this ghost shit. Listening, I allowed myself to go back down memory lane with them. We had some good times. When Paradise started talking I wanted to go hug her, but the devil in me said fuck that bitch she can eat a dick. I decided to finally speak up and let them know we were okay. The shit was getting depressing. After going over the plans and Nik ran off, I decided to go take a shower. I needed to get the fuck out of these clothes.

"Smalls let me get some jogging pants and a shirt. I need to take a shower. Suave don't wear shit but cardigans and slacks." Suave slapped me on my arm and I winced from the pain.

"You gone look real big in my shit. I may as well let you have it. Big ass gone stretch the shit out my V neck. You gone have that bitch looking like a U neck. Damn, let me find your ass some old shit." Laughing, I glanced at Paradise and kept walking. She can't tell because I only have one good eye, but I promise I was mean mugging the shit out of her ass. I jumped in the shower and allowed the water to cleanse my wounds. They had beat me so bad, the water hitting my wounds didn't even hurt. I was immune. I hope the swelling went down some by tomorrow, I needed to get back to how I normally look and I was tired of Smalls joking me out. I laid down getting my mind ready for tomorrow. Shit was about to get as ugly as I was looking. I told him, to put a bullet in my head. Now they would learn.

SUAVE...

Nik and Smalls argued all night long. I couldn't get no sleep in this mother fucker. I guess I could sleep on the plane, too much was on my mind anyway. Getting up to go in the kitchen I saw Paradise had slept on the couch. G needed to quit being an ass and talk to her, but I knew my brother wouldn't. His ass was stubborn as a fucking mule and right now his ass was looking like one too. Nobody in the house must have gotten any sleep because everybody started coming in the kitchen.

"Which one of yall ass is about to cook. I need a good meal before we go on this flight." Of course, that was Smalls hungry ass. Nik didn't say anything to him, she just started grabbing pots and shit. G walked in and he looked worse than he did last night. Blood was oozing out of his wounds, but the swelling did go down some. His face was black and blue from the beatings. My baby got up and grabbed a first aid kit.

"Come here G, let me fix you up." Tank was softening up to G finally.

"Nigga when that shit heals, I'm going to fuck your ass up again. Tank told me you stole on her ass."

"Snitches get stitches sis." He playfully hit her on the arm.

"Dummies do too." She tried to whisper it, but I could hear their conversation. "Gangsta, I don't know if your brother ever told you, but when I got out of jail I robbed his spot. Granted, I didn't know him or his homies, but that doesn't change the fact that I did it. Long story short, I made a mistake and killed Keem. The entire time we were dating, he was looking for the person responsible. When I got shot, he had just found out that it was me and the crew that did it. He was in the same mental as you. I am grateful every day that he chose to forgive me. The point I'm trying to make is, I know you are saying to yourself there is no way you and Paradise can be happy after a betrayal. Just look at us." She talked to him as she cleaned his wounds. Never wanting to go back to that day or remember anything that happened, I knew what she was trying to do. I had intentions on having this same talk with him myself.

"I hear you sis, but I'm not there yet. I need time to think. I love her, but I don't know if I can be with her after this. Hell, I don't even know if I want her to live after this. Ouch sis that hurt." I think Tank pushed hard on purpose.

"Tank hurry up and bandage that nigga up before his ugly ass drop blood in the food. I don't want to catch that shit. Mother fucker look contagious." Making everyone laugh, Smalls smacked on some bacon as we all waited on the rest of the food to be done. Having a family moment, it was good to laugh and joke before we made our trip, but now it was time to get it moving. We didn't need to give him time to think of a plan.

"Alright yall, we need to get out of here." Paradise walked out right on time. Tank had given her some clothes and shoes so that she could take a shower. This was probably the first time her and G had to ever wear somebody else's shit, but nobody had time to go home or back to hotels to get clothes. It was time to put an end to the bullshit.

On the way to the airport, I hit my nigga old connect up and told him what we were coming to do. I needed his crew to roll with us for back up just in case. I also needed for him to have us some weapons. We couldn't take ours through the airport.

"Remind me when I get back to buy a fucking plane. Before Tank I didn't travel and shit, but I can't be getting on no plane full of mother fuckers I don't know." I never thought I needed my own plane until now. Even though we were in first class, the shit was still uncomfortable. Niggas in suits looking at us like we are crazy. Maybe they were looking at G ass. I'm sure they thought we didn't belong. Little did they know they worked every day for a check and we could not lift a finger for the rest of our lives and still have money. Laughing at that thought, I decided to close my eyes and get some sleep.

****

Fully refreshed I was in go mode. My connect Ruiz met us at the airport. We decided to go to his spot first to go over a plan and figure out how we wanted to approach this. Columbia was definitely different from the states. One block you may see some run down houses that looks like huts, and then the next block is beautiful. It was high rises and huts basically. We rode through the city and up this long as hill it seemed like. Pulling up to his crib, I was glad Tank wasn't here. She would want me to buy a new house. It was a city block long. He punched in a code and we continued in. It took us damn near 5 minutes just to get up the drive way. I noticed there were no security around.

"You feel safe here without any men outside guarding the place?"

"Just because you don't see them, doesn't mean they aren't there." Waving his fingers, a red light appeared out of nowhere on my chest.

"Point taken, now tell him to take this shit off me. I don't like when niggas up on me." With the wave of his hand again, the red light was gone.

"Excuse me, do yall have any food in this mother fucker. Some fruit or something?" Ruiz looked at Smalls, but didn't answer. Walking us to the pool area a nigga could get in a lot of trouble here. It was naked women, food, drugs and anything you can think of just laying around. Smalls simple ass went straight to the food. Gangsta must have been trying to piss off Paradise as he stared blatantly at the women.

"Okay let's get down to business." Ruiz noticed they were getting distracted. "Paradise do you have the layout of your father's mansion?"

"Yes, it's about 10 minutes from here. Kind of the same layout, but bigger. There will be men at the gate, on the roof, and porch. That's just the outside. They surround the entire compound. The key will be to take all of the guards out at the same time, but silently. If my papa feels he is under attack he will detonate a bomb to go off. There are a lot of tunnels and he will be safe from the explosion. This time of day he is usually siting by the pool, conducting meetings. If we are to attack now will be the time. Most of the guards will be there with him." Paradise looked at us as she gave us all the info we needed.

"Okay, men will take out the guards surrounding the compound to get you your way in. We have silencers, so drawing attention won't be the problem. Once we get you in, we are done. We will meet you back here if you make it out safe. This is the code you will use to get in. Do not come here if you are being chased. Are we clear?" Everybody nodded and we suited up for war.

I was starting to think everybody in Columbia was rich. Paradise's home was twice the size of Ruiz's mansion. We followed the truck to the front of the house to make sure we had access. The rest of the cars split up to take their position. Waiting for our que, we stayed in until they cleared the premises. You couldn't hear the shots, but the bodies started falling out of nowhere. We stayed put until we saw the trucks and cars pulling off. That was our signal, they had done their parts. Moving quickly, Paradise punched in her code and just like that we were in. We didn't want to run into any more guards, so we went around the house taking the long way. Reaching our destination, we assessed the situation first. Wanting to see how many guards they had and where he was positioned. We didn't want him to get away and detonate the bomb. It was 10 guards and he was sitting at the table with Sin's bitch ass. We were going to be able to get a 2 for one. I got so excited my dick got hard.

"This is how we will do this. Me and G are going to take out the guards. Once we start shooting, Paradise run to your father immediately. Don't allow him the chance to get up. Smalls you go with her, but you keep your gun on Sin. Don't leave them room to sneeze and nigga don't kill him. We have a special death for his ass."

"You niggas always on some sick shit. I just want yall to know I'm not cutting off no balls and shit." Smalls whispered causing us all too laugh under our breath.

"Everybody ready? We go on 3." I looked around to make sure everybody was good. I couldn't tell if Gangsta was or not because I was on the side with the bad eye, so I just started counting.

"1, 2, 3." Me and G stood up and started taking they ass down with precision. Out of the corner of my eye, I saw Smalls and Paradise moving. One thing about me and my brother, we didn't have to let off a bunch of bullets trying to hit someone. We were a perfect shot. Dropping all of the guards in 7 seconds flat, we walked over to the table to join the others.

"Yall having a meeting without us? Do you mind if we join you?" I sat at the table with them like I was invited.

"You are a disgrace to our family. Look at you, all of this over some gutter ass nigger." I noticed he said nigger and not nigga. That's what the problem was, Louis was a fucking racist.

"Correct me if I'm wrong, but wasn't Journey's mom black? I guess it's okay for you to fuck a nigger, but not your daughter." Smalls asked while he grabbed food off their plate.

"I don't even care what you think anymore. You talk about loyalty, but you allowed him to hold me hostage, you paid my sister to fuck my man, and then you threw it in both of our faces. You don't know shit about loyalty. See you were dealing in feelings and didn't you tell me that makes a person weak. You know how the Garzon family is, we don't do weak." Paradise yelled as she sent 5 bullets into his head. Ready to get the fuck out of dodge, I grabbed Sin up by his arm.

"Let's go pretty boy. We have something special for you."

"Fuck you, yall may as well kill me now because I ain't going nowhere with you mother fuckers." Sin thought he had an option. *Bam.* The nigga body went limp in my arm. Dropping his arm, I allowed him to hit the floor and looked over at G to see why he hit him.

"Nigga I didn't feel like chasing or dragging his ass. He said he wasn't going and we have to get the fuck from out of here." Gangsta explained.

"Well, get to dragging then. " Walking off, Smalls followed behind me and Paradise helped G. Once we got to the car, we sped off like we were being chased. I was just happy that everybody was coming home safe and now we could put this all behind us. Killing Sin was the last piece to the puzzle and this nigga was about to experience pain like never before.

GANGSTA...

Once we got back to Ruiz's mansion, I prepared to set up for what I had planned for Sin.

"Ruiz, do you have a horse stable here on the property?"

"Yes I do, but you will have to drive to it. I don't think you would want to drag him that far. Driving, it's only about 5 minutes. Do you need my men to assist you in anyway?"

"Naw, I'm good. I don't think your men want to see this shit anyway. It's about to get ugly and a lot of people don't know how to stomach how I choose to kill."

"You don't have to tell me, we have heard many stories of the great Lucifer. Why do you think I didn't ask if you needed my help?" I couldn't do shit but laugh. Everybody knew not to fuck with me, that was a good thing. I thanked him and walked off to get the others.

"I'm about to drive to the stable and set up, yall can bring this nigga over in about 10 minutes. I got in one of Ruiz's cars and headed to the stable. Getting out I grabbed the things that I needed. Walking through the stable, I checked each horse to see which one would be perfect. Satisfied with my choice, I led him out and tied him up to the wall. Grabbing the roll of gauze, I began wrapping it around the horse's dick. This mother fucker was big as hell. I'm glad I wasn't a horse, how the fuck they take this big mother fucker in the ass was beyond me. I had to use 2 rolls in order to fully cover the big ass dick and then I moved on to the next step. Grabbing the double sided tape, I started wrapping that shit around his dick as well. I guess he hadn't had none in a while because he was excited as hell. Dick was flapping everywhere.

"Calm down boy, I ain't with that funny shit." Like the damn horse could respond, I held a full conversation with his ass. Now, for the final step. First I squirted super glue on the tape to give it some extra hold. Then, I grabbed the bag of glass that I had and started sticking it to the tape. Once I was sure that I had enough glass and that it wouldn't come off. I waited for them to bring Sin in. After 10 more minutes went by, I started to become inpatient. Then I got worried that maybe he got away. Running out of the door, I saw them pulling up. This time, Paradise, Suave, and Smalls dragged his ass. Taking his rope to the top of the stable, I tied one end up to the fixture that was hanging from the ceiling. Making sure it was tight I came back down. Then I tied his hands. I put the rope in a double knot so the nigga couldn't get away once the pain started.

Handing each of them a pair of gloves, I gave out my instructions.

"Do not allow any of his blood to touch any open wounds you may have. Do not get close enough to him, I don't want him to be able to scratch or bite you. I'm not sure if you all know, but Sin is HIV positive. Be careful dealing with him."

"Aww hell naw. This nigga was a flaming fairy? Why the fuck didn't you tell us that before? I just drug his ass in here and shit." Smalls started scratching like I said he had bed bugs.

"Just put your gloves on and be careful."

"You don't have to tell me twice." Smalls pulled his gloves on so fast he almost busted them.

"Are we about to wait for him to wake up or what?" Suave was ready to get the show on the road.

"Nope, we are going to wake him up. Hold his head up and his mouth open." I knew Smalls wouldn't, all he ever did was watch when me and Suave did our killing. Once my brother had his head up and mouth open, I walked the horse over to him and placed his dick in his mouth. After giving it a couple of tugs the horse started bucking like crazy. The glass cutting his mouth made the nigga wake up immediately.

"I'm glad you are still with us. I didn't want you to miss your own party." When he realized he had a horse's dick in his mouth his eyes got big as hell. Suave grabbed him by his head moving it back and forth to ensure that he sucked the horse off.

"You thought you could fuck my girl, kidnap her, shoot my brother, and then try to kill me? You don't cross the devil. You kill him. Suave that's enough, it's time for phase 2. After we took the horse's dick out of his mouth, the horse got pissed. He wanted his nut, and I was about to give it to him. "Stand him up." Suave pulled him up and I pulled his pants down. Blood was pouring from his mouth and the bitch was crying.

"Please don't do this. I'm sorry. I let jealousy get the best of me and I shouldn't have. You killed my mother, sister, and her daughter. I haven't killed anybody. Can we please be even?" Everyone looked up at me shocked. They didn't know I had took out his family. I would answer questions later, right now I had business to attend to.

"You are right, I did do all of that. Did you know I fucked your mama and your sister before I killed them? Your mama was terrible and she was ugly as shit without her wig, but your sister. She was the real MVP." Paradise looked uncomfortable hearing this, but I didn't give a fuck about her feelings right now either. "At least you all can be together now. I'll put your mama wig in the grave with you, so you can give it back to her when you see her." Smalls busted out laughing. That nigga can't ever be serious. I turned his body around, to make sure the horse had easy access. Guiding him over I placed the horse's dick at the tip of Sin's ass and allowed him to go to work. The damn horse didn't even try to slide it in slow, he went straight for the kill. He was tearing Sin ass apart. All you saw was flesh and blood. I allowed the horse to get his nut before I stopped the assault. I pulled the horse away from him.

"Good boy. Did that feel good? It's okay you can go to sleep now." *Bam.* I shot the horse in the head.

"Nigga what the fuck you killing the horse for? It's this tweety bird looking ass nigga we supposed to be shooting." Smalls looked to me for answers.

"He has HIV Smalls. The horse was going to die slow. Suave make sure you tell your homie I'll compensate him for the horse." Turning back to Sin, I wanted to complete what I started. I took the hammer out of the bag and began hitting him on his ankles. Not stopping until they were completely crushed. His screams were so loud, I just knew Ruiz and them could hear him way at the house. Grabbing the saw, I chopped his feet off.

"If you were going to chop the nigga feet, why did you hit them with a hammer first?" Smalls ass had a lot of questions.

"With my parents, we had an electric saw. Smashing his bones makes it easier to cut." This time Paradise walked over and hammered at his knees. She knew the process, we had done it too many times before. We completed this until we had his entire body chopped up.

"I swear I'm going to stop fucking with you niggas. What is wrong with yall. Paradise, now I see how you were able to stay with this nigga. Bitch you crazy too." Smalls walked out of the stable. We were done and Suave pulled his gun and shot him in the head twice.

"Nigga what the fuck are you shooting him for. They done chopped his body up." Smalls walked back in when he heard the gun shots.

"Tank said Mz Lady P brought everybody back to life and I wasn't taking no chances."

"Who the fuck is Lady P?" Everybody asked at the same time.

"I don't know, but the bitch is crazy." We laughed and jumped back in the car. Once we got back to the house, I allowed Suave to talk to his man. They were close.

"Ruiz, you are going to need a clean up crew in the stable. Also, we had to use one of your horses. Shit got messy and I had to put it down. I will compensate you for everything. No matter the cost." Suave explained.

"Unless you are coming back in the game, your money is no good here. Go home and be with your family."

"Thank you, but I'm done. Can we get a ride to the airport?"

"Sure. But Suave, you have too much money to be flying commercial. Buy yourself a plane."

"I already know." Heading to the airport, I felt good that our family was heading back home as a unit. The shit was finally over. No more wars, no more searches, and no more beef.

11- HOW DEEP IS YOUR LOVE

"Are we living a lie baby, is the magic gone. Do you feel the same way you used to? Girl tell me if it's wrong to love like this. How deep is your love?" Keith Sweat

TANK...

I was going to kill my husband and his crew when they get back. I have been calling them and leaving messages none stop. Nik is in labor and she is not a happy camper. This bitch is going off on everybody because Smalls is not here. Bitch said she is not going to push until he walked in the door. Calling them again for the umpteenth time, the phone went straight to voicemail. I don't know what's going on, but I'm going to fuck they ass up when they decide to finally grace us with their presence.

"Excuse me Lashay." It was the doctor trying to discuss the issue with me.

"I'm trying to locate her boyfriend now."

"I'm sorry, but we are prepping to perform a cesarean on her. She won't push and she is going to harm the baby." Fuck. Why did I have to be the one to deal with this shit. Walking in the room, I tried to talk some sense into her.

"Friend, if you don't push, they are going to cut the baby out. You don't want that."

"They can do what they feel they have to, but I'm not pushing until he gets here."

"Nik, I know you are scared, but you are harming the baby." She turned her head away from me and I knew that meant she wasn't giving in. The doctor came in with some orderlies and they started pushing the bed out. They were about to do a C- Section. When Smalls came running in and almost tripped over the bed.

"I'm here baby. I made it. Where is she going?"

"They were about to cut the baby out because she wouldn't push." He looked at me in horror.

"Doc, you don't want to do that. You see my friend over there? He like to cut people too, but he don't have a license. Would you care to meet him?" Smalls didn't crack a smile.

"It's okay doctor, I'm ready to push now." Tears were rolling down her face. I'm sure they were happy tears.

"Okay, if you are not the mother or the father I need you to exit the room." We all left out and I noticed that Paradise was really quiet.

"What's wrong sis?" She looked at me and allowed the tears to flow.

"You're pregnant, she is in labor, my sister is somewhere out there pregnant with my man's baby, and G don't want anything to do with me." My heart ached for her, but I could give her some peace.

"Journey is not out there anywhere. I killed her and that ugly ass baby." She hugged me and cried on my shoulders. I knew I had made the right decision when I killed that bitch. Paradise was too much like me and I know I'm not raising another bitch's baby.

"Sis, everything will work itself out. You just have to believe. He will come around. He just needs some space." Nodding her head at me, I hoped G got it together quick, but for now I was waiting to see my God baby.

SMALLS...

When the plane landed, we kept our phones off because we wanted to surprise our girls, but to our surprise they weren't at home. We walked through the door and was met by dead silence.

"Where the hell could they ass be this time of night?" Suave was thinking out loud.

"Knowing the Supremes, they ass probably on a flight to Columbia ready to have a shoot out." G laughed, but me and Suave looked at each other and grabbed our phones quick. As soon as we powered them on, all kinds of alerts were coming through. The first text I saw said *Nik is in labor if you don't bring your black ass home, I'm gone be the pappy.*

"Oh shit, my girl in labor let's go." I listened to every message as we sped all the way to UIC Hospital. "Man she is going to kill me if I miss this birth. Gangsta I need you to drive faster. Why the fuck is this nigga driving anyway and he got one eye?" I decided to put my seatbelt on. Suave was laughing, but he won't be if his ass get hit. We finally got to the hospital, G barely parked the car before we jumped out running through the doors.

"Labor and delivery please."

"Sir, who is the patient?"

"Nikita Towns."

"Okay 4th floor room 106." We took off running again. When we got to the room Nik was crying and they were rolling her out. I was so happy I came and was able to stop them from cutting on my baby. I missed the birth of Ariel and I was excited to see this one.

"Come on Nikita push." Nik started grunted and I could see some hair coming out her pussy.

"Okay push again. Right now." The grunting started again and now the pussy was stretching so wide, I couldn't believe it. When the head came out, I was done. Ain't no way I'm competing with that shit. How are we going to have sex after this? The baby done ruined my damn pussy.

"One last push. Push now." The body came sliding out and a nigga couldn't do shit, but cry. They took the baby over to the sink and cleaned it off.

"Congratulations. You have a beautiful son." Nothing could have ever prepared me for this moment. I leaned down and kissed Nik a million times.

"Here is your baby boy." The nurse handed him to Nik and I swear he was perfect.

"Baby, he got more hair than you." She slapped me and I couldn't do shit, but smile. "I'll be back. Let me go get everybody else." I walked out to the waiting room and my family was sitting there with every damn balloon and bear from the gift shop.

"Yall want to meet yall nephew?" They didn't even respond they jumped up and ran to the room. Standing there smiling like a damn pedophile, I looked over to Paradise and she looked sad as fuck. I wanted everyone to be happy on today. It was not a day for sadness. I walked over and grabbed the baby from Tank.

"I see we are gone stay fighting." She pouted, but when she saw me walk over to Paradise, she started smiling with me. Handing her the baby, I had never seen Paradise light up like this. She started rocking back and forth and singing to the baby. Everybody got mesmerized in her voice. This was a great moment and I was the happiest nigga alive.

SUAVE...

Seeing Paradise with the baby at the hospital broke my damn heart and I wasn't going to sit back any longer and allow my brother to make a fool of himself. When we got back to the house, I told him to come down to the basement and holla at me. The girls stayed upstairs. Smalls and Nik were still at the hospital.

"You know you are fucking up right?"

"I don't need any more lectures, I got this."

"You may have this, but you won't after a while. That girl loves you, but a person can only take so much."

"I know, but I don't know if I can get pass her fucking Sin."

"You have to my nigga. Forgiveness is not for her, but it's for you. I'm not telling you something I don't know first hand. Have I ever been wrong before?"

"No."

"Okay then. Listen to me baby brother, you are going to regret it if you don't. Forgive her and move on." He didn't respond, but I know I got through to him. "Now, I'm going upstairs to get some pussy. I suggest you do the same. I walked upstairs and found my girl. Come here baby, somebody want to talk to you." She got up smiling and damn near ran to the room. I picked her up and tongued her down. Let's go take a shower together. Once we were clean, we climbed into bed and I just held her for a moment.

"Thank you Lashay."

"For what bae?"

"For following your heart and saving me two times. I know I am hard on you, but I don't ever want to go through that feeling again of almost losing you and I understand that's why you did it. If it wasn't for you and your girls, none of us would be here today. So, thank you.'

"Thank you for that." She leaned over and started kissing the tip of my dick. "Because you are an awesome husband." More kisses on my tip. "I'm retiring my gun. No more rah rah shit from me. I am going to allow you to lead and I will follow." More kisses. "Just know if you ever need me to, my gun is always locked and loaded." Then she deep throated it. There was no better feeling than this right here. I felt sorry for anybody that has never experienced it.

GANGSTA...

When my brother and his girl left to go fuck, it made it awkward as hell for me and Paradise. I didn't know what to say to her. Before I could think of a way to break the ice, she went running in the back to one of the guest rooms. I gave her a minute and it also gave me time to figure out what I wanted to say. I finally got up and walked in the back to see if we could try and mend what had been broken.

I heard the shower going and I walked in the bathroom. She was sitting on the shower floor butt ass naked and crying. This is something I never wanted to see. I always tried to give her me in the way I knew how, but that was not enough for her. What if she felt it wasn't enough again? Would she hire someone to kill me the next time? How could I ever trust her after this? I didn't know the answers to these questions, but what I did know was that I loved her. She was my everything. I knew that as her man I had fucked up. I made her feel unwanted and I had to accept that I played my part in this as well. We both fucked up and we both had to be willing to try again. I didn't know if our love was strong enough to pull us through this like it did for my brother and his girl. But I did know I was willing to try. I removed my clothes and climbed in the shower with her.

"Don't cry Paradise. We will figure it out." That only made her cry more. I leaned down and allowed my lips to touch hers. She looked up at me and this was the first time I ever saw her scared. Standing her up I grabbed a towel and started washing her body. I did the same for me and rinsed off. Grabbing her hand, I led her out of the shower and laid her on the bed. Grabbing her pussy with my mouth I went to work. Sucking, licking, and swallowing all at the same time. I have craved this for so long and now I had it. Pushing her legs back so I could get a better angle, I continued to work on her pussy.

"G I missed you so much. Damn baby. Yes, just like that." I didn't need guidance, I knew her pussy inside and out. Right as she was about to cum, I got up and slammed my dick in her. Gasping as I continued to assault her, she grabbed the sheets to hold on for this ride. Spreading her legs apart, I used her ankles as leverage and continued to slam all of my dick into her pussy. I pulled out and used her legs to flip her over. Pulling her back to me, I slammed my dick back inside. Gripping her ass cheeks to pull them apart, the sight of me going inside the pussy I loved made me brick hard. Using my thumb to caress her asshole, I pushed it in with no warning. Now fucking her with my dick and my thumb, Paradise started going crazy. She was throwing it back so hard, I almost nutted. I pulled my thumb out and stuck two fingers inside her asshole. That only caused her to fuck me harder. I was trying to prove a point. I needed her to know the only dick she would ever need is mine. Trying to be in control I slid another finger inside her. Fucking her ass with the same aggressiveness I was fucking her pussy, she started screaming and them BOOM. She fucking squirted. I guess her and Journey were sisters after all. I literally lost my mind in all of her juices that was going everywhere.

"baby I'm cumming. Oh shit I'm about to cum again." Before I could try to gain control. BOOM. She squirted again. I could no longer hold back. I released all of me inside of her. Laying down beside her, I felt we could now talk since I had broken the ice.

"Paradise, I know it's been a lot of hurt on both of our parts. I just want to apologize for my side of things. I wasn't trying to replace you. The hurt of you being gone was too much to bear and I had to fill the void. I was fucking losing it out here. A nigga was going crazy. I couldn't even sleep. When I met her, that was the first time I had slept in 3 days. I just wanted to feel close to you. I didn't think she was better than you. A nigga slipped up. The first time we had sex I thought it was you. I'm telling you a nigga mind was fucked up.

I have never felt hurt like that before. By the time I realized what I had done, it was too late. I know that don't excuse what the fuck I did, I just want you to know it wasn't intentional. I also know that my actions pushed you to another nigga, but that can't ever happen again. If you feel like I'm not enough or what you want, then leave me. I will probably kill you before I let you go, but try that way. Don't do no fuck shit like this no more. Or I promise I will kill you where you stand and grieve your ass the next day."

"G, I am sorry. I didn't know what else to do. Part of me just wanted your attention. The day you came over to Sin's house I was in the closet. I heard and seen how you was about my disappearance and I knew then I had made a mistake. I tried to back out of it, but Sin's bitch ass hit me over the head with a gun and knocked me out. I woke up hand cuffed.

He did some bad things to me and that's on me. I deserved every bit of it. Just know that it will never happen again and I am truly sorry. I know I hurt you and I don't ever want to see that look on your face again. We both have to make some changes, but for now I'm just glad I have you back. Oh, and if you ever put your dick in another bitch, I will cut you up and leave you in our freezer. I will play dumb about where you are and be eating on your ass every night."

"Now that's some sick shit." Mugging me in the face, she leaned up to kiss me again. I guess God does answer prayers from the devil. I'm not perfect and she ain't either, but we are perfect for each other.

SMALLS…

I could not stop staring at my son. I was trying to see who he looked like. I think he got his mama looks more, but he definitely got my hair. Even though Nik was still pissed at me, this was the best day of my life. I knew that this was the perfect time to try and make up with her lil head ass.

"Baby, you did good. I'm proud of you." She just stared at my ass. "Look you can sit here and keep acting like a kid or we can talk. Either way I'm going to sleep well."

"You already knew how I felt about leaving the first time and then you turn around and leave again. I thought your ass was dead and you walk right in the door saying you leaving again. How fucked up are you."

"Look, I thought you had hair when I met you, but did I get mad when I found out your ass was bald headed? No, I loved you anyway." I did get a smile out of her with that one, but I was dead ass serious.

"Smalls can you ever be serious? You can't make those kind of decisions by yourself."

"I am the head of this house hold girl. I did what I knew was best for our family. You need to get over this shit. I'm home, I'm alive, and I'm happy. Quit trying to take that away from me."

"I'm not trying to take it away, I just don't want to lose you. I know what you do for a living and I have accepted it, but don't cross me out like I don't have a say so. Don't treat me like your child. Treat me like I am your woman." I pulled out my phone and sent a text. I could tell that pissed her off. "This nigga texting while I'm trying to talk to his simple ass." I laughed because I knew she would feel differently soon. Everybody walked in the room and she got irritated. I knew she wanted to finish our conversation. I stood up and responded to what she had just said to me.

"I don't want to treat you like you are my woman." Her head snapped around so fast the bitch looked possessed. Suave handed me a box. "I want to treat you like you are my wife. I love your bald headed ass and I want you to always know you are my partner forever. Will you marry me?" She started crying immediately.

"Yes, baby I will." All you could hear was aww all around the room. She stuck with a nigga through all his bullshit and now she is stuck with me for life.

EPILOGUE...

SUAVE...

Life was good and we had been back in Hawaii for months now. We went back for Nik and Small's wedding, but we got our ass back on our plane as fast as we could. Yes, I said our plane. I bought one as soon as everything was over. I missed running the streets and everything about it, but nothing beat the feeling of knowing your family is safe and nobody is after you. The family was all standing around my living room watching Tank ass give birth to my son. She wanted a home water birth and made everybody stand here and watch. I wasn't too comfortable with everybody seeing my wife's pussy, but it was what she wanted. Thinking this may not have been a good idea as I watched her struggle to give birth. She was in so much pain and wouldn't stop crying. I couldn't do anything to help her or take the pain away. I looked to the mid wife for answers.

"Is everything okay? Is this normal all the pain she is in?"

"Sometimes. I'm about to check her now to make sure the baby is okay." She stuck her hand up Tank's pussy and began to check around. Pulling her hand out, she looked at me and shook her head. "The baby is breached. He wants to come out feet first."

"What does that mean? Doc talk to me." Everybody looked on in horror.

"It means that the cord could be around the baby neck and if she pushes him out, he could die. I may have to give a C-Section."

"But I haven't taken any meds doc." Tank cried. I had no idea what any of this meant. All I knew was my baby was in danger.

"I know and if I perform it without meds, you may not make it. I don't know if you will be able to take the pain."

"Doc, I have to have faith in God in a matter like this. We are going to proceed. Just please make sure my baby is okay." The doctor started prepping to deliver the baby. Everybody was hugging me. I stood there in tears wondering what was going to happen. The doc stuck her hand in Tank and started giving instructions.

"When I tell you to push I need you to do it okay."

"Okay." Tank cried.

"Push." The doctor's hand was still in Tank, so I couldn't see anything. "Push." We looked on, but nothing changed. "This time I need you to give me a big one. Push Lashay." My baby grunted with all her might and out of nowhere the doctor brought her hand out and there was my baby boy. She cleared his mouth out and slapped him on the ass. There was no sound, and then there it was. The prettiest sound I ever heard in my life.

"Congratulations on your baby boy." I grabbed him and started kissing him. Blood and all.

"Hey little man, I see you wanted to start some shit already. I'm your daddy. Hey little man." I looked over at Tank and she was sitting in the pool looking up at me just smiling. "Tank if you don't get your ass out that pool and put some clothes on, I'm going to beat your ass."

"Shut up silly, we have to wait for the afterbirth to come out." I don't know what that shit is, but I needed her to get dressed. I gave the baby back to the mid wife and allowed her to clean him up. I was kissing Tank when this big ass red block came sliding in the water.

"What the fuck is that? If that's another baby I'm not claiming his ass as my nephew fuck that." Smalls was looking in disgust.

"That's the afterbirth." The mid wife laughed as she passed me the baby back.

"I was going to wait to tell you mother fuckers, but yall got a nigga all emotional." Gangsta started speaking to the room. "Paradise is pregnant." While everybody congratulated them, I saw my brother ease down on his knee. I had to be seeing shit. There was no way possible my brother was proposing.

"Paradise from the first day I met you, I knew I would do anything in my power to keep you. We have been through some rough times, but we made it through. All it took was for you to get kidnapped for me to see how much I was fucking up." The mid wife mouth fell open. "I don't ever want to lose you again, unless it's because I killed your ass. So, will you marry me?"

"Fuck yeah." We all laughed at Paradise. The room was now passing the baby around and congratulating G and Paradise at the same time. Our family had made it out and I was grateful. Looking over at Tank, I knew I was right about her the first time I met her. I knew she would be mine forever.

"Tank, the damn liver looking shit done fell out. Now put some damn clothes on before I beat your ass."

THE END...

PLEASE LEAVE A REVIEW AND TURN THE PAGE FOR A SNEAK PEEK OF LATOYA NICOLE'S HOOVER GANG: CASH RULES EVERYTHING AROUND ME COMING SOON.

BLAZE...

"Damn baby, suck this clit. Right there. Don't stop daddy." This bitch was getting on my nerves with all this talking.

"Bitch I know how to eat pussy damn. Now can you nut so I can stick my dick in? I got somewhere to go." Looking at me like she wanted to say something smart, she thought better of it when I looked up at her. My eyes were a pretty grey, but them bitches was ice cold.

"Fuck I'm about to cum. Yes, baby. Yes." Her body started shaking and I couldn't be happier. Grabbing my condom, I slid that bitch on and slid my dick in her now ready pussy. As soon as I got inside of her I knew this was a mistake. This bitch pussy was loose as a goose. When I tell you I didn't feel nothing, I didn't feel shit. It felt like my ass was fucking air. Slamming my dick inside her, I tried moving my hips side to side to feel something. This bitch started screaming for dear life.

"Oh God, this dick is so fucking good. This is your pussy baby." She knows damn well she didn't feel my dick because I couldn't feel that mother fucker. If I didn't already know it was there I would have thought I lost that bitch in the waves. I started slamming my dick like crazy and shuddered some. Faking a nut because I needed to get up out this bitch right now. I rolled over like I was wore out and she had the best shit ever.

"Too bad I gotta go, I was gone give you an all nighter." Smiling at me I got up and threw my clothes on. Removing the condom, I stuck the shit in my pocket.

"Why you doing all of that baby, I have a garbage can." She looked offended.

"I know baby, it's just something for me to keep until I see you again. I gotta remember this good pussy." This bitch looked shaky. Like she might try to turkey base my shit. "I'll call you later after my meeting." I kissed her on her jaw and went to walk out of the door.

"Hoover nobody, does it like yooouuu." Did this bitch really start singing the vacuum commercial? Simple bitches. Laughing, I damn near ran out of her shit. I had to take one for the team, I needed the key to the vault. But somebody else was gone have to start dealing with these hoes.

OTHER BOOKS BY LATOYA NICOLE

No Way Out: Memoirs of a Hustla's Girl

No Way Out: Return of a Savage

Gangsta's Paradise

THANK YOU TO ALL OF MY READERS AND SUPPORTERS. PLEASE READ AND REVIEW. I LOVE YOU ALL.

LATOYA NICOLE

CPSIA information can be obtained
at www.ICGtesting.com
Printed in the USA
LVHW082350230119
605046LV00039B/744/P

9 781547 057245